Mango
All the Time

Mango

All the Time

BY FRACASWELL HYMAN

STERLING CHILDREN'S BOOKS
New York

STERLING CHILDREN'S BOOKS
New York

An Imprint of Sterling Publishing Co., Inc.

STERLING CHILDREN'S BOOKS and the distinctive
Sterling Children's Books logo are registered trademarks
of Sterling Publishing Co., Inc.

Text © 2022 Fracaswell Hyman
Cover art © 2022 Frank Morrison

ISBN 978-1-4549-3395-3
ISBN 978-1-4549-3397-7 (e-book)

Distributed in Canada by Sterling Publishing Co., Inc.
c/o Canadian Manda Group, 664 Annette Street
Toronto, Ontario M6S 2C8, Canada
Distributed in the United Kingdom by GMC Distribution Services
Castle Place, 166 High Street, Lewes, East Sussex BN7 1XU, England
Distributed in Australia by NewSouth Books
University of New South Wales, Sydney, NSW 2052, Australia

For information about custom editions, special sales, and premium
and corporate purchases, please contact Sterling Special Sales
at 800-805-5489 or specialsales@sterlingpublishing.com.

Manufactured in Canada

Lot #:
2 4 6 8 10 9 7 5 3 1
11/21

sterlingpublishing.com

Cover design by Gina Bonnano
Interior design by Christine Heun

—

To Jamaya, Vernicia, Jackelin,
and all the friends of Mango
who have reached out.
I appreciate you!
—F. H.

—

CHAPTER ONE

Up, Up, and L.A.!

$\mathcal{E}$ ver since I drowned my ex–best friend Brooklyn's phone, my life has been one surprise after another. Brooklyn tried to play a dirty trick by signing me up to audition for the school musical. I auditioned because I didn't want to let her plan to humiliate me work, and guess what? I was cast to play Juliet in the school musical *Yo, Romeo!* I never wanted to be an actor, and sure, I could sing, but I never thought I'd sing in front of anyone besides my bathroom mirror, and then *BOOM*! I'm playing the lead in the musical.

The show turns out great; I have a lot of fun, make new friends, and discover my passion for being onstage; and then . . . another big surprise. I'm cast in an Off-Off-Off-Broadway version of *Yo, Romeo!* and spend the summer in New York City costarring my friend/crush, TJ, which is great. Unexpectedly, TJ gets replaced by my favorite star (next to Beyoncé, of course), Gabriel Faust! He turns out to be kind of a jerk and quits the show, which leads to us closing early.

. . .

Two days after I returned home from New York the ground was shifting underneath me again and I was leaving home. This time I was headed for Los Angeles for a screen test. If I passed the test, I would be cast in a show starring my favorite TV star, Destiny Manaconda! The weirdest thing of all the weird things that were happening in my formerly ordinary twelve-and-three-quarters years of life was that Destiny Manaconda was now kind of a friend. I mean, we'd met in New York when she was hanging out with her pretend boyfriend, Gabriel Faust. At first she was cold and distant, but later I grew to like her as a person, not just a TV character. I guess she grew to like me, too, because she was the one who recommended her high-powered manager, Maxwell Paige, approach TJ and me with a deal to fly us out to L.A. to test for a chance to play her friends in a new TV show.

Back in New York, Destiny had kind of warned me about the pitfalls of being a star. How hard it was to live up to your image and keep your fans interested in everything you do. How you had to be disciplined and give up fun things that might affect your job. How lonely it could be working so hard and being so young. So there was a part of me that wasn't completely sure I wanted a new, weird kind of Hollywood life. I mean, I liked being regular Mango: hair pulled back in a big Afro puff with a scrunchie; T-shirt, jeans, or jeggings; hot Cheetos; and pepperoni/pineapple pizza (yeah, I know a lot of people hate that, but I live for the salty/sweet combo). I liked being home with Mom and Dada and my little teddy bear brother, Jasper. I missed them when I was away. Still I said yes to the chance to experience a new adventure.

"Yes" is such a strange word. "Yes" is great when someone says yes to you. "Mom, can I stay up late?" "Dada, can I have some money to go to the mall with my friends?" "Hey, great and wonderful best-parents-in-the-world, can I have a dog?" When yes is the answer to any of those questions, you feel great! (Actually, no was the answer to the dog question, because Mom said our apartment was too small. ☹) But then there are the times when someone asks you to say yes to something, and you have to make a decision, and the decision you make will come with responsibilities and sacrifices. "Can I borrow your green-checked Vans?" "Can you watch my baby sister while I can run to the store?" "You're good at math; will you help me study for the test?" "Will you come to Hollywood and take a screen test that could make you a star?" Saying yes to any of these questions can turn out to be quicksand that pulls you under, and there is no escape, only regret.

Since the trip to Hollywood was only supposed to be for two days at the most, Dada was coming with me. He had just finished catering a fancy vow-renewal party for my wealthy friend Hailey Joanne's mother and father. It was a great success and the biggest job Dada's new catering company, Delicious Delights, had handled yet. He worked so hard to make it a success, and he deserved a rest, so my parents

3

decided he should go with me. It would be both Dada's first time in California and mine. Dada was just as excited as I was; I could tell by the sparkle in his almond eyes. "I can't wait to sample authentic West Coast cuisine, Mango-gal. While you're busy screen-testing, I'll be busy eating and finding new ideas for my catering company!"

It was before sunrise and time to head to the airport. Maxwell Paige had sent a car for us, so we said goodbye to Mom upstairs in our apartment. Jasper was sound asleep when I kissed him on his soft, peach-fuzz cheek. He had grown so much in the weeks I'd been in New York. He could even pronounce "Mango" clearly now. I have to admit, I kind of missed the way he used to say Mamo-Mamo all the time.

Heavy clouds hung ominously low in the sky, and thunder rumbled in the distance as we climbed into the town car. Not exactly ideal weather for taking off in a plane to fly across the country. I snuggled in close to Dada as we pulled away from our building. I felt a tingle, a sort of electric current running through me, as I thought about heading for a new adventure. The "tingle" was both positive and negative, because anyone who has ever read an adventure knows that there are downsides and upsides. Unexpected obstacles you have to confront and overcome . . . or not. Challenges you weren't exactly prepared for that you must conquer . . . or not. You always hope things will turn out all right. Sometimes they do, and sometimes your hopes float away like dandelion fluff. I'd had my share of roller coaster adventures over the past year. Was I ready to face more ups and downs? I sighed and thought, *Ready or not, here I come.*

When we arrived at the airport, TJ was there waiting. Maxwell Paige had sent a car for him, too, but no one accompanied him. TJ's Mohawk hair looked smooshed to one side, like he hadn't tried to do anything with it since he woke up, but his kiwi-green eyes and smile were bright. I was so happy to see him. TJ was sort of my boyfriend . . . or the closest thing to a boyfriend if I had one. I mean, if you break it down, he was a friend and a boy, but not just a regular friend. TJ was a boy who *like-liked* me and I *like-liked him* . . . but he was not an actual boyfriend.

Anywho, TJ's mother agreed to let Dada chaperone him on the flight across country, since she was busy preparing for her wedding to a man who would become TJ's stepfather. TJ didn't come right out and say it, but I had the feeling he didn't care for his mom's fiancé very much. TJ wasn't the type to talk a lot about his home life, but if you listened closely to his songs, you could tell what was really going on in his heart. He did tell me that he was looking forward to spending time with his biological father, Malachi Gatt, a corporate lawyer who lived and worked in L.A. It had been almost a year since he'd seen his dad in person.

A weird thing happened at the gate as we were about to board. When the agent called for priority and first-class passengers to begin boarding, Dada, TJ, and I walked forward and were first in line. (Maxwell Paige had the producers arrange first-class travel.) The gate agent smiled and said, "Sorry for your misunderstanding, but this call is for *first-class* and priority passengers only. Step back, and we'll call you with your group."

A red-faced man behind us carrying a garment bag sighed and started to move around me. Dada put up his hand to the man, saying, "Hold on, please, sir." He turned to the agent and showed the tickets on his phone. TJ showed his phone too. "I believe we have seats in the first-class cabin. Group One, if I'm not mistaken."

The agent blushed, cleared her throat, and said, "Oh, of course . . . I just . . . People often make mistakes and . . . *uh* . . . welcome. Go right ahead and board." The whole thing was so weird and awkward. As we walked down the jetway to board, I asked, "What was that about?"

Dada shook his head. "Never mind. Just ignorance, that's all. Forget about it." He smiled and winked at me, but something about his eyes told me he wasn't brushing it off as easily as he asked me to.

Heavy raindrops were beating against the airplane window as we buckled our seat belts. Dada let TJ and me sit together in the two comfy leather seats in the second row of the cabin. He sat in the aisle seat directly across from us. This was a very different flight from the one I had been on earlier in the summer. The seats were way wider, and I actually had room to stretch my long legs. Dada fell asleep as soon as he sat down. TJ was quiet and kept fiddling with a guitar pick, rolling it from finger to finger.

"Wasn't it kind of embarrassing being stopped at the gate like that in front of everybody?"

"Yeah, but I think she wound up more embarrassed than we did."

"Why?"

"Because, she just assumed we didn't belong in first class because . . . well, you know."

Yeah, I guess I did know, but it wasn't something I wanted to talk about or think about. I started checking all the gadgets on the armrests. A thing to turn on the lights, a button to call the flight attendant, USB ports to charge your phone, and a little tray you could slide out to hold a cup. I couldn't help but notice TJ kept fidgeting with the guitar pick. I nudged him, "Are you nervous about the screen test?"

"No."

"About flying in the rain?"

"Uh-uh."

"Really? I am. How could you not be?"

He shrugged. "People fly in the rain all the time. Once we get above the clouds, it'll be a smooth trip. I've taken this flight before."

I gulped as the engines revved and the plane lurched forward and started picking up speed streaking down the runway. I wanted to reach for TJ's hand, but then I'd disturb his fiddling with the guitar pick, so I clenched my fists and decided to keep talking to take my mind off my nerves.

I pulled the window shade down and turned to TJ. "I'm kind of nervous about the screen test. I'm like so not a fan of tests anyway. And now, we're gonna be tested on a screen. You know, like on TV? It's gonna be like awk-weird to the max, you know? Not like doing a play where there's a separation between the audience and the cast. With TV, cameras can zoom in really close, and people can see your zits."

He looked at me. "I don't have any zits, do I?"

"No. No you don't. I'm just saying . . . you know, it's different, and I just can't understand why you're not nervous."

"Well, it's not like being on a TV sitcom is something I've always wanted. If I get on the show, cool. If not, I guess that's cool, too, but . . ." He trailed off and didn't speak for what seemed like the longest ten seconds ever, then he said, "I'm kinda hoping things go well with my dad and he wants me to move in with him though."

"You mean for good and not go back home?" This was a shocker. When we were in New York, TJ and I had confessed that we *like-liked* each other. We'd promised to hang out a lot and maybe even become girlfriend and boyfriend down the road. Now, to find out he wanted to stay in California? It felt like a tiny crack was forming in my heart. Like a fault line that could signal an earthquake.

"I'd go back home maybe for visits," he said, "but my mom is starting a new life, and I don't want to be in the way."

"Did she say you were in the way?"

"No, of course not. My mom is great. She loves me."

"What about her fiancé?"

"Mitch? I don't know. I think he wishes I weren't there. He never says it. Not in words. But you know, I can kind of feel it when I'm around." He lifted the guitar pick to his mouth and started gnawing on it, kind of like the way I chew my fingernails when I'm nervous. "My mom doesn't want me to live with my dad though."

"Because she'd miss you?"

TJ leaned his head back and closed his eyes. "Yeah, that too. I don't really want to talk about it, Mango. We'll just see what happens."

Seems like we both had things we didn't want to talk about. I didn't want to talk about why we were stopped before boarding the plane, and TJ didn't want to talk about how his mother would feel about him moving away. I guess some things were just too tender to deal with for both of us.

I felt bad for TJ, and even though I didn't want him to move away, I hoped his father would at least *want* him to stay. Although he'd cut the conversation short, it was a good distraction from my fears. I lifted the shade and looked out the window, and TJ was right: we were high above the clouds, and the sun was shining bright, reflecting on tufts of snowy white cotton balls below us.

CHAPTER TWO

LA-LA Landing

When we landed at LAX (that's the code for Los Angeles International Airport; where the 'X' comes from, I have no idea), it was a long walk to the arrivals area. We each had one carry-on rolling suitcase, so we didn't have to go to what's called the luggage carousel. I giggled to myself when I heard that, because I imagined a carousel where you rode on suitcases instead of horses. Actually that could be kind of cool. There'd be small rolling bags for the little kids; for bigger kids there'd be larger suitcases, steamer trunks, and duffel bags, and you could choose whatever you'd like to ride on. I think I'd choose a steamer trunk, because it'd be fun to get inside and ride around and around.

When we reached the transportation area, there was a crowd of people waiting. In the midst of them we spotted a man with a long white beard and a white ponytail. He was wearing short pants and a shirt with palm trees on it. He kind of looked like Santa Claus on vacation. Vacay Santa was holding up a sign that said "Mango/TJ." TJ and I looked at each other and smiled. "You think he's here for us?"

TJ said, "Nah, there's probably a lot of Mangoes out here in California."

"Yeah, well, what's the T and J for?"

Dada laughed and said, "Tall Jamaicans, of course!"

TJ laughed. I rolled my eyes. Dada was so silly with his corny jokes. He waved to the Vacay Santa, saying, "Hey there, we're the ones you're looking for."

"Oh, so you're the new stars?" He held his hand out to TJ and me and gave us both a really strong handshake. "Nice to meet you. My name's Arthur Tablachefski, but everybody calls me Tabby. I've been assigned to be your driver during your stay here in L.A."

Dada said, "Nice to meet you, Tabby. I'm Sidney Fuller; this is my daughter, Mango; and this young man here is TJ."

"Great. How are you, young fella?"

"Um, I'm okay . . ." TJ kept looking around, "I thought my dad was gonna meet me here, but I guess he couldn't make it."

"Maybe he'll meet us at the hotel." Dada nodded reassuringly at TJ. "He's probably waiting there now."

"If that's true, he'll have a long wait," Tabby said. "I'm supposed to take you all directly to the studio. You'll probably be there for a few hours if things go the usual way. There's a lot to cram in on this short visit. Come on, let's see if we can beat some L.A. traffic."

Tabby led us out of the airport to my first glimpse of L.A. sunshine. The light felt brighter than what I was used to. The buildings gleamed, reflecting the sun, and all at once I understood why Californians seemed to always wear sunglasses.

We waited outside under an overpass while Tabby went to fetch the vehicle. There were hundreds of people coming and going—kind of like in New York but different. Things didn't feel as rushed here, but it still felt like people were anxious to get where they were going.

A white passenger van pulled up in front of us, and the door slid open. Tabby called out, "All aboard!" I have to admit, I was a little disappointed as we got in. I mean, I knew I wasn't a star, but I thought we'd be riding in one of those big SUVs with the blacked-out windows like Gabriel Faust rode around in. Guess you had to be a bigger star to rate one of those.

We arrived at the entrance gate to Chrysalis Studios, one of the few actually located in Hollywood, according to Tabby. The guard waved us through, and Tabby drove us straight to the entrance of Stage 13, and who should be standing there waiting but the man who could possibly become our new manager (if things worked out), Maxwell Paige. As we climbed out of the van, Maxwell Paige's lean brown face broke into a big grin. "Welcome! How was your trip?"

"It was nice, Mr. Paige," I said.

"Max. Call me Max. I insist. All my favorite clients do."

I wasn't sure how we came to be his favorites so fast since we hadn't done anything or actually signed with him yet. Maybe that's the way people related to each other in Hollywood. You know, "Love ya, babe!" "You're the best!" "You're gonna be a star!"

TJ and I nodded. "Okay, Max."

Max turned to Dada and thanked him for chaperoning us, then said he wanted to show us the soundstage where we would be doing the screen test in the morning, "And I'd like to introduce you to the creator and executive producer of the show."

"Now?" I said. "Shouldn't we go to the hotel and shower and change first?" I was wearing shorts, a Stranger Things T-shirt, and my favorite orange hoodie, which was a little frayed around the sleeves but I loved because it was so comfy.

"That won't be necessary," Max said. "You see, I have a master plan. I want the powers-that-be to see you two as regular, everyday kids, because that's exactly what they're looking for. Trust me, I got you!"

I looked from TJ to Dada and back to Max and shrugged. "Okay, if they won't mind my travel stink, let's go."

As we headed into the soundstage, TJ leaned close and said, "If I'd known this would happen, I would've taken a shower this morning."

I leaned away from him. "*Eww*! TMI!" We laughed.

CHAPTER THREE

Ring Around the Soundstage

S oundstages are HUGE!!! This one was the size of maybe two or three airplane hangars. My eyes popped open when I saw how incredibly vast it was and how incredibly small it made me feel. I just stood in one place with my eyes wide and my mouth hanging open as I turned round and round, taking it all in.

There were several sets all around us. The interior of a bank, a gym, a bedroom, a living room, a home office, a two-car garage, and a backyard with—I couldn't believe my eyes—a swimming pool! On another side of the soundstage was a high-tech laboratory next to what looked like the surface of an uninhabited planet surrounded by a giant green screen. On one side of the planet was half a huge spaceship that looked like it had crashed into some boulders! High above there were grids of catwalks where lights were hung and poles with hanging backdrops that were painted to look like real streets. My eyes met TJ's, and his eyes were bugged out, too.

Max said, "This is the set for a film that was just completed. They're going to use it for your screen test before it's torn down."

"They tearing this down?" Dada said. "We could move in here and pay rent. It looks so real!"

"Movie magic, Mr. Fuller."

"Look bruddah, if the kids can call you Max, you can surely call me Sid, yes?"

Max smiled and nodded, and they bumped fists. "Sid it is."

From far across the soundstage we heard "Hey there! Hi! Sorry I'm late."

A girl was running at top speed toward us. She came to a stop and took a moment to catch her breath. She was the same height as TJ, wearing blue camouflage cargo shorts, a green Chrysalis Studios sweatshirt, red sneakers, and horn-rimmed glasses (the kind that have a thick frame on top but metal wire along the bottom). Her hair was cut in a high-top fade with blonde-tipped twists at the tips. She was the same coffee-brown as Dada and I were, and she had a bright white smile with a gap in her two front teeth. It was a very friendly, likable, and smart face.

My first thought was that she was another actor who was going to play a kid on the show. Maybe she and I were there to test for the same part. Max held his hand out toward her. "I'd like to introduce you all to Dionne Harmony." He turned to us. "These are the kids that are testing tomorrow. Mango Delight Fuller and TJ Gatt."

15

Dionne smiled and held out her hand. "Hey, what's good?"

I shook her hand. "Hi, Dionne. Are you doing a screen test, too?"

Max and Dionne looked at each other and chuckled. Dionne said, "I don't have to do a test; I created the show. I'm the executive producer and show runner."

"Show runner?" Dada said. "What's that?"

Max chimed in. "It's means she's the boss."

TJ and I spoke at the same time. "You?!"

Dionne snickered and nodded. "Yep. Me."

"But you look like a kid yourself!" Dada held up his hand and said, "Sorry, I didn't mean anything by it, but, well, you could be Mango's teenage sister."

"No worries, Mr. Fuller. I can't help how my genes have favored me, but be assured, I am an adult. I've been writing and directing series TV for a few years now. Now, finally, I've got my own show."

TJ said, "Wow! That's crisp."

"Super crispy!" I gushed. "What shows have you worked on?"

"Well, my last writing job was head writer on *Cupcakers*."

I yelped and actually leapt off my feet. "*Cupcakers*? That's my number one favorite show in the history of the world!" I couldn't stop talking, my mouth was moving at warp speed, and I was making wild gestures with my hands, "*OMGZ*! Wait 'til I tell Izzy! This is too cool! You just don't know how much I loved that show! Is that how you know

16

Destiny Manaconda? Of course, it is! How could you work on that show and not know the star? Wow! Me and my friend . . . actually my ex-BFF, Brooklyn, we used to—"

TJ put a hand on my shoulder, "Mango."

"Huh?"

"Reboot. You're uber-fangirling right now."

He was right. I was shaking and close to screaming and crying the way girls did in old Michael Jackson concert videos. This was not cool. I was grateful for TJ's help putting on the brakes. "Oh no, I'm sorry, uh . . . note to self, embarrassing!"

Dionne laughed. "Please! No need to be embarrassed. Actually, it's pretty rare for a behind-the-scenes person like me to get that kind of reaction. You made me feel like Destiny for a minute there. I appreciate it."

Max said, "Should we head to your office, so you can talk to the kids?"

"No, that's too stuffy. You know what? I just finished directing my first movie on this set. How about I show you around, and we can get to know one another while we tour?"

TJ and I nodded eagerly.

Max said, "I'm going to take Sid away to talk show *business,* and we can all meet up at the commissary for lunch."

"Bet." Dionne said. As she walked away, TJ and I followed. I stopped when Dada said, "Mango, this all right with you?"

"Of course, Dada." I reached up and kissed his cheek. "I'll see you at the commentary."

Max said, "CommisSARY."

"Oh yeah, that too!" I giggled, waved, and jogged to catch up with Dionne and TJ.

Dionne showed us around the set, telling us about her movie. "It's a comedy about a teenage boy who finds out his parents are aliens from another planet who adopted him when he was an infant. He finds their spaceship, accidentally takes off, winds up on the planet his family came from, and has to start a new life where he is now the alien."

I thought that was way crisp! TJ and I asked questions about the sets and cast, and before you knew it, we were just having a conversation about all kinds of things.

I was trying hard not to fangirl again, but when Dionne asked if we wanted to climb up on the spaceship set, I started jumping up and down and clapping. Even cool-as-ice TJ was psyched by this. We sat in the crew chairs on the spaceship and pretended to do a launch sequence and take off into space.

Dionne called us over to the garage set and explained that this is where we would do our screen test the next morning. "This is not the actual set we'll use for the series, but it's close enough."

"The show is about a garage band, right?" TJ said.

"Yes, a garage band with Destiny, the lead singer, and a few of her friends backing her up. That's where you come in if everything works out."

"I've seen shows like that before," I said. TJ gave me a look, and I realized that what I had just said could be taken as an insult, like saying Dionne's idea wasn't original.

Dionne smiled. "Not necessarily like this. You see, Destiny's character sings, but she can also time-travel."

"What? Like to the past?"

"To the past and to the future. The funny thing is, she can't control it. She never knows when it's going to happen. She feels a twitch in her eyes, and suddenly she's in Salem, Massachusetts, about to be burned at the stake for being a witch, or in Paris, France, five hundred years in the future sky-surfing during a meteor shower!"

I gasped. This was so exciting! "Do her friends get to time-travel, too?"

"Not exactly, but they appear as different characters wherever she pops up. So you might be playing Cleopatra's Egyptian handmaiden in one episode or a futuristic cyborg in another."

I turned to TJ and involuntarily punched him in the arm. "I can't even!"

"Ow, Mango!"

"Sorry, but isn't this is amaz-tastic! I can't wait!"

"Uh . . . we haven't gotten the gig yet."

"Oh yeah." I looked at Dionne, who was watching us with a broad smile. "Would you mind if I got some footage of you two hanging out on the house set?"

I looked at TJ, and we both shrugged and nodded yes.

Dionne took out her phone and started filming. "Just hang out like you're at home. Explore the set."

TJ and I giggled as we walked around the "kitchen." Opening cabinets and the fridge, commenting on what we saw. Making up stuff as we went along. Pretending to make breakfast with the fake eggs and super realistic bacon. It was so much fun.

When we were exploring the garage, I noticed a couple of bikes hanging on the wall. I turned to Dionne. "Are those bikes real? Can we ride them, Dionne?"

"Yeah. This place is huge; ride around if you want."

"Okay!" We lifted the bikes down and took off all around the soundstage. We rode around the perimeter, which was about a half mile or more. Riding across the planet set was bumpy but fun. We zipped in and out of the machines in the lab and raced down streets. Heading back to the house, I called out, "Last one in the backyard is a cow pie!"

The race was on. I took off and quickly pulled ahead of TJ. I was sure I was going to win. Pedaling as fast as I could, I turned back and stuck out my tongue. "Nice try, cow pie!"

TJ yelled, "Mango, look out!"

I turned to look ahead, and before I could stop, SPLASH! My bike and I were in the pool! Luckily, it was a movie pool, so the water was only about three feet deep. TJ and Dionne rushed up, asking if I was all right. I stood up, completely drenched from head to toe, and I couldn't help it, I started laughing. Then TJ started laughing. I splashed water on him and was completely surprised when he jumped into the water and started a splash war. It was the most fun I'd had in my entire life!

We noticed Dionne still filming us with her phone and laughing, too. She said, "I think it's about time we headed to the commissary."

"Like this? We're drenched!"

"It just so happens," Dionne said, coming toward us with a big grin, "this is a movie studio, and we have a wardrobe department with over a hundred thousand costumes. I'm sure we can find something you can borrow."

TJ and I gave each other high-fives and climbed out of the pool. As we headed toward the soundstage exit, leaving wet footprints across the floor, TJ and I peppered Dionne with questions. "Do you think I could wear a genie costume?"

"Do you have like a knight's armor that could fit me?"

"Oh! What about one of those Marie Antoinette dresses with the really high wigs?"

"What about a gladiator?"

"Oooh, yeah, I wanna be a gladiator, too!"

Dionne laughed, walking backward while still filming us as we headed to the wardrobe department.

When we arrived at the commissary (that's movie studio for lunchroom), TJ and I were both dressed like gunslingers from the Old West, complete with cowboy hats, boots, and chaps.

Dada and Max laughed at us, but we fit in just fine. There were lots of people in costume all around us having lunch. Dada and Max were more out of place than we were.

When Tabby arrived to take Dada and me to our hotel and TJ to his dad's house, Max gave us our screen test scenes. "Study hard and work on memorizing your lines this afternoon. We can go over the scenes at the dinner party tonight."

"Dinner party?"

"Where?"

"With whom?"

"Oh, didn't my assistant email you?"

I didn't know. I was having so much fun, I hadn't checked my phone for hours. When I checked, it was still on airplane mode. Max went on, "Destiny is throwing a dinner party at her home to welcome you to Los Angeles tonight. I thought you knew."

A grin stretched my lips to the far sides of my face. Imagine, arriving in Hollywood, playing in a pool on the soundstage, better and better!

CHAPTER FOUR

The Valley Arms

My first day in Hollywood was full of firsts: entering a ginormous soundstage for the first time, meeting an African American woman writer/director/producer, hearing what the TV show was about and how cool it was, falling into a three-foot-deep fake swimming pool and having a splash war, getting to wear a full-on authentic Wild West movie costume. Still, there was another first waiting just outside the door of the commissary.

Under the electric blue sky with the dazzling Hollywood sunshine, TJ shouted, "Dad!" He rushed over to the curb where two men were waiting next to a black Tesla parked in front of Tabby's van. I wasn't sure which of the men TJ was referring to, but when he embraced the taller, darker-complexioned man, I knew that was his dad. I saw they had the exact same face, except the dad was much darker than TJ and his eyes were brown, instead of TJ's kiwi green.

They hugged for a long time, and I wasn't sure, but I thought I saw TJ swiftly wipe a tear from his eyes when they let go. TJ turned to the guy next to his dad, and they did a quick, sort of back-slapping, friendly hug, then TJ waved Dada and me over. "This is Mango and her dad, Mr. Sid. This is my dad, Malachi, and his husband, Ezra." Ezra was shorter than TJ's dad, but they shared the same complexion. His hair was cut short and his eyes, nose, and lips were more pronounced.

Okay . . . *outside time* continued to move right along as usual with introductions, handshakes, and stuff. TJ's dad, Mr. Malachi, talked about how much TJ had spoken about me and how happy he was to finally meet me. All through these usual pleasantries, my *inside time* was a tad out of sync. I didn't know TJ's father was married to another man! Why hadn't he told me? Then again, why should he have told me? Was it a big deal? I wasn't sure, but something about it felt kind of like a big deal to me. We all said our goodbyes and how much we looked forward meeting again at Destiny's dinner party later that evening.

As Dada and I got into the van, I noticed TJ get into the front seat of the Tesla with his father. His expression was so full of smiles and warmth. They were obviously very close. No wonder TJ was hoping to move to California.

As we headed for the hotel, Dada told me about his meeting with Max. "This is quite an opportunity, Mango. If you get this part, your weekly pay per episode will be more than your mother and I earn in a month combined and then some. We'll have to sign a three-year contract with what they call 'options.' You would have to live in Los Angeles for a good nine months of the year while shooting the series."

"What about school? Would I go to a new school here?"

"Not while you're working. You'd have a tutor and take classes on the set while the show was in production. It'd practically be a whole new life for you . . . for all of us."

"Would you and Mom and Jasper move here?"

Dada sighed and shrugged. "I don't know, Mango-gal. That's something I'd have to talk over with Margie. Would that be to your liking?"

I shrugged. "This morning, I wasn't really worried about getting this job. I mean, I thought it would be fun to see Hollywood, but mostly I wanted to get back home and start school with my friends . . ."

"And now?"

I looked out the window as we sped by palm trees with the mountains in the far distance. "I don't know. It's been such a fun day. Dionne is really cool, and her idea for the show is so fun and exciting. I guess now I kind of want to do it really bad."

"Well, Mango-gal, all you can do is do your best. We'll put a pin in the rest of it until we have to decide one way or the other."

"Okay, Dada." I pulled the screen test scenes out of my back pocket where I had stashed them. "Guess I'd better start working on these."

As I was unfolding the scenes, I almost asked Dada what he thought about TJ having two dads, but I decided not to. Dada didn't seem surprised or taken aback or anything, which was cool. Besides, I thought I ought to talk to TJ about it first. I didn't want to feel like I was talking about him or his dads behind their backs.

With L.A. traffic, the hotel was about an hour away from the studio in a place called "the Valley." Tabby said, "The Valley Arms is a pretty nice place. Comfortable rooms with kitchenettes. Most of the families who bring their kids out here for pilot season stay there."

Dada said, "Pilot season? What's that?"

"Oh, that's when all the studios produce one episode of a show they think has potential—usually the first episode. They film it, then decide if they're going to pick it up for a series. Mostly it happens around this time of the year. The parents who have kids who want to be actors and who are talented bring them out to Hollywood to audition. Some get a series or a commercial or a one-off role. Most don't, but they come back each year, like geese flying north for the spring."

"Are lots of kids around my age staying there?" I asked.

"Your age, younger, older, a whole mishmash of wannabe superstars. I get to drive some of 'em back and forth, day in and day out. You know Destiny Manaconda? I drove her and her family back and forth for a few years before she hit it big the third year they came out for pilot season. At least ten years ago, I think. She was just a little bitty thing the first time I laid eyes on her. About six years old, quiet and shy. But look at her now, huh!"

So Destiny started auditioning for pilots about ten years ago, when I was two years old. I wondered how many trips I'd have to make to get on a show. No. I decided this would be it for me. If I didn't get cast in this show, I'd just go back to my normal life, hanging with Izzy and the rest of the drama-nerds at Trueheart Middle School. But then I looked down at my scenes, thinking about the fun day I'd had so far. To be honest, I wanted to pass this screen test and get this job. The more I admitted it to myself that I wanted it, the more the mango pit in my stomach that grows heavy when I'm nervous or anxious started to grow. My fingernails began to tingle. I wanted to chew on them, but I knew Dada would give me "the look" if I did and say, *Mango-gal, that's a nasty habit to get into. Move ya fingers from your mouth before I have to dip them in Scotch Bonnet pepper sauce.*

The people at the front desk of the Valley Arms were all ready for us and showed us to our room right away. It was nice and smelled like a lot of cleaning products—which I'm sure Mom would've appreciated. There was a small living room that had a flat-screen television and a balcony that looked out over the pool. There were lots of kids swimming and splashing and hanging out by the water. The kitchen was tiny but clean. There were two bedrooms, and each had a queen bed, a dresser with a mirror, and a good-size closet.

The one bathroom was on the small side, with bright pink tiles from floor to ceiling, pink flamingos on the shower curtain, and was loaded with towels, soaps, shampoos, lotions, and a handheld hair dryer.

After checking the place out, I plopped down on the bed in my room, the one that overlooked the pool, and curled into a ball, holding my stomach. Dada came into the room with my suitcase. He sat at my bedside. "Mango-gal, what-a-gwan?"

"Nothing."

"Nothing? Me know it's somethin' when you ball up like a Mongolian soy curl. Now tell Dada. Are you just tired from the trip?"

"Yes, that too."

"What else?"

"I really want to pass the screen test and get the part, but the more I want it, the more my stomach hurts."

"Why so?"

"Because, if I don't get it, I'll be so disappointed, and if I do get it, it might mean a major upset for our whole family."

"Mango-gal, no need to worry your mind so."

"But I am worried."

"Me muma used to say, 'Worryin' is like waterin' a field of yam when ya don't even have the seed.'"

I smiled, even though I wasn't sure what it meant. I just liked it when Dada pulled out these obscure sayings with the thickest parts of his Jamaican accent. Still, even without yams, the mango pit in my stomach was getting heavier by the second.

"Tell you what," Dada said, "you've got a lot of preparation to do, but you won't be able to do your best unless you're relaxed. So let's put on our bathing suits and spend an hour or so at that pool they got out there."

As soon as Dada said that, I started feeling a little better. Dada went to his room, and I opened my suitcase and pulled out my favorite, a blue crop-top bikini. But where was my swim cap? I couldn't find it. I yelled across the hall, "Dada, I can't find my swim cap!"

"That's okay."

"No, it's not! I can't get my hair wet. Mom would kill me if I didn't wear a swim cap."

Dada returned to my room, went to the closet door, opened it, and looked inside. He got down on his knees and looked under the bed, then he started opening all the drawers. I said, "What are you looking for?"

"Your mom. She ain't here, as far as I can tell, so she can't kill you for swimming with your hair free!"

I sighed. "That's so corny. But we have a dinner party tonight, and I have the screen test in the morning. I can't risk messing up my hair!"

"Did you notice there's a shower in the bathroom and shampoo and a hair dryer? Go swim free, gal. When we get back, shower and wash your hair, and I'll blow-dry it. Problem solved. Genius Dada strikes again!" He walked out of my room strutting like King of the Roosters.

I laughed and began changing into my bathing suit. I had the kookiest, smartest, best dada in the world. I was excited to spend an hour in the pool, letting my worries float away with the water.

CHAPTER FIVE

How NOT to Make a
Big Splash in Hollywood

Dada and I found a couple of deck chairs in the sun and claimed them with our towels. Dada stretched his arms wide, looking up at the sun. "You know, Mango-gal, the weather here is the closest I feel to being back in Jamaica since I've been in the States."

I smiled up at him. "Guess that means you like it here?"

"Me like the tone of the sunshine and the warmth without all that mugginess we have back home."

I hadn't noticed, but it was true. There was almost no humidity, even though it was warm. I pulled off my scrunchie, and a gentle breeze blew my hair around my face. Dada sat on the edge of the pool and I joined him, our long limbs dangling in the water. The pool was very large, and there were kids and mostly moms all around. Little kids on one side in the shallow end. Fewer people in the deeper end, where there was a long diving board. Most of the moms were gathered at tables under umbrellas, scrolling on their phones, playing cards or backgammon, or just hanging out. It seemed as though they were all friends. Dada and I were strangers to them, the new kids in town, and I could tell by their glances that some of the parents were sizing up the competition.

On the other side of the pool, there were two girls around my age, one Black and one White, sitting close to each other, their feet dangling in the cool water. I noticed them because it seemed like they were looking at me and then whispering back and forth. The Black girl had her hair in box braids that fell down her back. The White girl's hair was red and shoulder length, and she wore a beach hat with a wide floppy brim. They looked at me, giggling, and quickly turned away when our eyes met. I decided to check myself before I started feeling some kind of way. I thought, *Mango, don't jump to conclusions and get an attitude. You don't know these girls. You don't know what they're talking about. Why should they bother you?* I took a deep breath and gave myself a *Hey Queen!* salute in my mind. It was much better to stay positive and concentrate on what was important to me, like relaxing and having fun with Dada.

"The water feel nice, yes?" Dada said, reaching down and splashing me. "You ready for a swim?" I nodded yes. We stood and jumped in.

I swam from one side of the pool to the other, then swam underwater. When I came up, I had to shake my hair to get some of the water off. It felt great to be able to swim without a tight cap over my ears and stretching my eyes. I don't think

I'd been able to swim like this since I was a toddler, and back then I couldn't swim. Mom always had the swim cap at the ready when we'd go to the beach or a pool. Most of the time the swim cap didn't even work and my hair got wet and matted anyway.

Dada swam up to me, "I'm going to the lobby to get a bottle of water. You want something to drink?"

"Yes, water please. Ice cold."

"You got it."

As Dada headed for the lobby, I just relaxed by the side of the pool, enjoying the feeling of the coolness of my body underwater, my head above, the sun shimmering on the blue water, the sound of kids laughing and splashing all around. I smiled to myself. *If this is California lifestyle, I'm here for it!*

I noticed the whispering girls climbing the ladder up to the diving board. The Black girl went first. She stepped to the edge of the board, kind of bounced a bit, lifted her arms up over head, and swiftly leapt. She barely made a ripple as her body sliced into the water like an arrow. Wow! I was beyond impressed.

The red-haired girl left her hat on the ground by the ladder, climbed up, and stepped onto the diving board next. This girl took her time approaching the edge. She had a more athletic build with broad shoulders that suggested she was good at gymnastics. She took a few steps backward, then charged toward the edge, leapt high into the air, did a sum-mersault, and plunged into the water like a rocket. My heart was beating so fast watching them. They were amazing. All of a sudden, I wanted to try it. This had already been a great day of firsts. Why not try squeezing in another?

I climbed out of the pool and walked directly to the diving board and climbed the ladder. I didn't want to hesitate or give myself time to *think it over*. Sometimes you just had to go for it without pausing to psych yourself out.

Up on the diving board, a little crust of hesitation began to form around the edges of my courage. I was much higher up than I thought I'd be. At least, that's how it looked at the top of the ladder. The diving board vibrated as I stepped toward the edge. The sparkling blue water below looked miles away. My eyes swept across the palm trees surrounding the pool, and for some strange reason I wondered why I didn't see any coconuts. All the sounds faded away, and there was a high-pitched buzz in my ears. A cold sweat broke out on my fore-head, and goose bumps popped out all over my arms. I was just about to turn back when I noticed those two girls looking up at me and whispering to each other. Were they waiting to see if I would chicken out? Would they laugh if I walked back to the ladder and climbed down on my soggy penne pasta legs? Something inside told me not to back down. It was like the feeling I had when I was tricked into auditioning for *Yo, Romeo!* Even though I didn't know them, I wasn't going to let those two girls see me run off scared.

I took a deep breath. Lifted my arms above my head and bounced on my toes the way I'd seen the first girl do. Just as I was about to dive I heard "MANGO!!!!" I turned to see Dada coming out of the lobby holding two bottles of water. The look of fear in his eyes made me want to abort, but it was too late. I lost my balance and fell, flailing my arms and legs and screaming. It seemed like I was moving in slow motion as I landed on the water belly first—OUCH! The next thing I knew, I was underwater. I knew how to swim, but I was so disoriented and in so much pain, I just kept flailing and going deeper and deeper. I had swallowed water, so as hard as I tried, I couldn't hold my breath. There was no breath.

Everything around me got quiet. I could hear my heart thumping loud and fast in my ears. I stopped flailing, because couldn't control my limbs anymore. I kept sinking. Like a rock. Then, I saw arms coming toward me, reaching for me. Two arms. Four arms. Six . . . fade to black. End of Mango.

CHAPTER SIX

The Drowned Girl

When I came to, I was in Dada's arms. He was rushing to our deck chairs. Calling my name. "Mango! Mango-gal, you're all right. Dada's got you. Mango, open your eyes, please, baby!

I opened my eyes, coughing and spitting up water. I didn't dare stop to think what was in the water I swallowed. Lots of people get lazy and relieve themselves without leaving the pool. *YUCK*! When Dada saw my eyes open, the stress on his face made a slow retreat.

When he placed me in the deck chair, I noticed a crowd had gathered around. Kids were gawking. Moms were sighing and shaking their heads with hands over their hearts. One ultra-dramatic little girl was sobbing, like I was someone very close to her who had died. I felt like I was under a microscope being studied and scrutinized. It was all too much. I hid my face in my towel and burst into tears.

Dada spoke to the crowd, "It's okay, folks. She'll be fine.

Just a little scare, but she's okay. Thanks for your concern. Appreciate it. Thank you."

Everyone walked away, except for the manager of the hotel. He asked to speak to Dada. Dada turned to me. "Just lie still, Mango. Catch your breath. I'll be right back." He stepped a few feet away with the hotel manager.

The two girls who inspired my diving misadventure came forward and sat down on either side of me, each taking one of my hands in theirs and patting it.

The girl with the long box braids said, "Sis, you like to scare me to death!"

"Me too! Feel my heart." The hat girl put my hand on her chest. "It's still beating like a jackhammer!"

"I'm glad my lifeguard training kicked in." Box braids swiveled her neck as she spoke: "When I saw you up there all wobbly, I knew I'd have to be Rescue 911 ready!"

"*Mm-hmm*! Me too! Especially after that belly-flop you did!" Hat girl held up her palm and high-fived her friend. The mention of belly-flop bought my attention back to my sore abs. I removed my hands from the two girls and rubbed my stomach.

"Oh, you poor thing. I hope you don't get a belly bruise. Those are the worst of the worst!"

"You can say that again—but please don't!"

These girls were obviously close, because they spoke alike and shared the same kind of mannerisms. It was as though two grown women had inhabited the bodies of twelve- or

37

thirteen-year-olds. They kept going on and on, talking about how they'd met years ago at the Valley Arms, coming out for pilot season. How they lived in different states, but they Face2Faced almost every day and traveled to visit each other when one or the other was in a show. Finally, I was well enough to say, "Who are you?"

Tickled, they looked at each other and ki-kied! Box braids said, "Oh, my goodness, Symphony, we haven't even introduced ourselves."

Symphony brought her hand to her mouth. "Kashara, girl, where are our manners?"

"I guess we were so busy rescuing you that we forgot to make proper introductions. She's Symphony, and I'm Kashara. What's your name?"

"Mango."

"Mango? Like the fruit?"

"Uh-huh."

After a brief but very noticeable millisecond pause, Symphony said, "That's so cute! Isn't that cute, Kashara?"

"*Mm-hmm*. Gwyneth Paltrow named her daughter Apple. And my daddy calls my mother Peach. It must be the new thing." They smiled at each other, then turned their smiles on me.

"You said you rescued me?"

Kashara raised her hand like she was in school. "I dived down first, 'cause I knew you needed help."

Symphony raised her hand. "Then your father came running across the way and dived into the pool like he was Tarzan or something. After that, I swam down to help."

"When we bought you up, girlfriend, it was like a scene from a movie. Everybody came running to see the drowned girl."

The drowned girl? Great. That's just the kind of tag you don't want hung on you when you get to Hollywood. I'd have to stay away from the pool for the rest of my time here. I could see it now. The minute I'd come outside in my swimsuit, people around the pool would watch and whisper, "There goes the drowned girl. She better keep her behind in the shallow section. She better stay away from that diving board and put a swim cap on all that hair!"

Kashara moved in closer to me. "So, what brings you out to La-La Land, Miss Mango?"

"I'm auditioning for a pilot."

A look of concern clouded Symphony's face. "Only one?"

"Yes."

"Which one?"

"Well, I don't think it has a title yet, but Destiny Manaconda is the star."

"Oh, I tested for that, and I have a callback!" Symphony said.

"They called you back already?" Kashara said, pouting. "I haven't heard anything."

"That's okay, girl. As long as you've done your best, there's no need to worry about it. Anything you can't control, let it slide, 'cause there's more opportunities on the other side."

"I heard that. Thanks, Symphony."

"You know I got you, Kashara."

Symphony patted my leg. "We are very supportive of each other. Girls have to stick together. Sisters have to uplift sisters! There is enough work to go around. No need to get jealous. Right, Kashara?"

"That's right. Last year there was a Midwest tour of *The Wiz,* and we both submitted audition tapes. Symphony got to play Dorothy, but I didn't get cast. Did I get mad and jealous? No way. I actually had my mama drive six hours so we could be there on opening night."

"And when Kashara was cast to play my dream role, Eponine in *Les Miz*, I was so proud of her. Even though a part of me was devastated, I was still happy for my best friend. Right, Kashara?"

"I didn't know you were devastated?"

"Oh, honey, I was. But I hid it. I used it as an acting exercise."

"*Ooooohhh!*"

Dada came back from talking to the manager. "Mango-gal, let's go up to the room so you can rest."

Symphony stood and said, "Can Mango have dinner with us tonight? We're going to a restaurant called Versailles. They have the best garlic chicken I've ever tasted in my life! And I do mean in my ENTIRE life! Right, Kashara?"

"Oh, you know it! I stan the garlic chicken of life!"

A bemused smile crossed Dada's face and he said, "Sorry, but we have dinner plans this evening. Mango, come." He picked up our towels and headed toward the lobby.

Kashara took my arm as I was leaving, "Where y'all going for dinner?"

"A dinner party at Destiny Manaconda's house."

Oh, why oh why did I say that? In the blink of an eye, the supportive *sisters uplifting sisters*, *we got you* feeling turned to a *girl-vs-girl*, *protect-ya-neck* glare. The way Kashara and Symphony looked at each other, then turned back to me, eyes narrowed and lips frowning. It was as though I had just pooped in their laps.

Kashara stood and flipped her long braids so they almost smacked me, "Well, you go on ahead, Miss Thang. Do you."

"Yeah . . ." Symphony said, "You go on and gather your brownie points, but it's talent that wins the day every time. Right, Eponine."

"Sure enough, Dorothy Gale!"

They walked away hand-in-hand and dived into the pool together like synchronized swimmers.

Well, I thought as I headed back to my room, *that was another first. The first time I'd turned fast friends into fast enemies in less than five minutes. A record. Hooray for me!*

I should have learned to keep my business to myself right then and there. But of course, I didn't.

CHAPTER SEVEN

Glass Houses

Dada ordered smoothies sent to our rooms to hold us over until the dinner party. I settled in, going over the lines for my screen test scenes. My role was a girl named Tempest, who is best friends with Destiny's character, Destiny. In the first scene, my character was trying to convince Destiny to help her hide a stray dog she had found. In the next scene, I was a sailor on the *Titanic* trying to convince Captain Destiny that icebergs weren't a problem in this part of the ocean. They were funny scenes. About three pages altogether and easy to memorize. I even tried a fake British accent for the *Titanic* scene. While memorizing my lines, I fell asleep and had a strange dream.

TJ and I were on the soundstage fooling around in the spaceship set when suddenly it took off. Destiny was the captain, shouting orders to us to help her navigate the spaceship. TJ was carrying out his duties like a pro, but I couldn't remember what I was supposed to do. Every time I pulled a lever on the console it turned to pasta! Suddenly, the space-ship, turning upside down and topsy-turvy, fell to earth and landed in a swimming pool on a strange planet. Six armed alien cats were battling us in a kitty litter splash war that we were losing when . . .

Dada woke me at six. My heart was racing, and it took me a moment to stop waving my arms as if I were splashing cat aliens. When I realized it was a dream, I quickly got out of bed, because I had to shower, wash my hair, get it blow-dried, and be ready for Tabby to pick us up at 7 for the drive to Destiny's house.

I'm not a girl who wears a lot of dresses, but Mom insisted that I pack at least one, and now I was glad she had. It was a light apple-green, stained glass–patterned summer dress with spaghetti straps, fitted at the top and flared out at the waist. I wanted to wear my sneakers, but Dada strongly sug-gested I wear sandals, which meant I had to polish my toe-nails. *Sigh* . . . Luckily, they sold nail polish in the lobby store. Dada dashed out and brought back polish that matched my dress. I polished my toenails and fingernails. Finally ready to go, I twirled around in the full-length mirror, and I must admit, I liked what I saw.

Destiny's house was on the other side of the valley, in the West Hollywood Hills. While Tabby drove, Dada told me about the phone conversation he had with Mom while I was napping. "She misses us, and Jasper keeps wondering where you've gone."

"I miss them, too."

"Me three. I mentioned the talk I had with Maxwell Paige. She was a bit concerned about the contract and the length of the commitment, but we agreed to think on it and talk about it when we were all in the same room back home."

"Did you tell her about what happened at the pool?"

"Do you think I'm crazy? That is a conversation best kept face-to-face, where she can see for herself that you're fine. Besides, I feel so guilty for leaving you alone in the pool even for a second."

"Don't feel guilty, Dada. It wasn't your fault. I just got caught up watching those two girls diving and making it look so easy. I just thought I could do it, and when I got up there, I got scared, but I was too proud to come back down. I should have, but you know me, my stubborn streak got the best of me."

"Well, well, well . . ." He nodded, an admiring smile spreading across his face. "You're getting very good at self-analyzing. Still, I'm going to make this right."

"How?"

"The next time we have access to a pool, I'm going to teach you to dive properly. Step-by-step. I don't want this mishap to frighten you away from a great sport."

"Do you know how to dive?"

"Ha! Didn't you know your dada was part dolphin?" He made a series of dolphin sounds that made me laugh, "*Ek-ek! Ek-ek!*" We spent the rest of the drive speaking "dolphin" to each other; eventually even Tabby joined in.

. . .

The streets in the West Hollywood Hills were very narrow and twisty. One lane each way, no sidewalks. From the street you couldn't tell what most of the houses looked like. No porches or staircases to the front doors. Mostly just walls with one door, tall fences, or thick bougainvillea hedges that kept the houses blocked from street view.

Tabby dropped us off at the entrance to Destiny's house and pulled ahead to turn the van over to the Valet Girls, a team of pretty ladies who parked the cars. They were probably actresses waiting for their big break. Before we could ring a bell or knock, we heard Destiny's voice coming through a speaker. "Hey, Mango, you're here!"

There was a long buzzing sound, and a latch clicked. Dada opened the door, and we stepped into another world. We were standing on a staircase that led down to a split-level house that seemed to be hanging off the hill and made of glass. On each side of the staircase were terraced gardens with fruit trees. Lemons, grapefruit, oranges, and tangerines. You could just reach out and grab one, they were so close and full.

A sweet fragrance that was so fantastic filled the air. I said, "What is that smell?"

Dada pointed to some low dark-green bushes dotted with delicate white flowers. "Those are gardenias you smell. My favorite flower."

I bent to take a closer sniff. "*Mmmmm!* Gardenias are gonna be my favorite, too."

We approached a sliding glass door. No. Not a glass door. A glass wall. There Destiny stood waiting, as the entire wall slid away, making what was inside become a part of outside.

Destiny hugged me. "Mango, I'm so glad you could make it."

"I'm glad to be here. You look amazing!"

Destiny, of course, was dressed to the nines. Her hair was now peach colored, her makeup was flawless, and her pantsuit, one hundred percent couture.

Dada said, "Thank you so much for inviting us."

"Of course, it's my pleasure."

"Is TJ here yet?"

"Yes, everybody's down on the south patio with the outdoor kitchen."

"An outdoor kitchen is a dream for a chef like me," Dada said. "Your garden is amazing. I haven't seen so many fruit trees since I left Jamaica."

"I've been very lucky. There are even more trees on the other side of the house. We have so much fruit that I donate most of it to the mission to feed the homeless downtown."

We stepped inside the house, where it seemed all the walls were made of glass, and you could see views clear out to the ocean to the west, and downtown L.A. to the east. I said, "This place is amazing."

"Do you want me to give you a tour?"

"Does a caterpillar want a cocoon? Of course! Yes!"

Dada said, "Would you mind if I check out the patio kitchen? It's sort of a dream of mine."

"Be my guest. Just go downstairs and follow the voices to the patio."

Dada gave a thumbs-up and headed downstairs, grinning like a kid on the way to collect presents under the Christmas tree. I followed Destiny, walking across an expansive living room with an enormous sectional sofa that faced another glass wall with a view of downtown L.A. There was a white grand piano in the center of the room. Huge abstract art lined the walls. I didn't quite get what the paintings were about, but the way the colors and textures were used stirred up feelings that I couldn't define. We passed through an indoor kitchen with a huge marble island and amazing top-of-the-line appliances, the kind that made Dada salivate when we watched cooking competition shows together on TV. I said, "You must love cooking in here."

"Cooking? What's that? Most of the time I use a food service that sends the prepared meals my nutritionist selects. My assistant, Mrs. James, pops them in the microwave, and I eat whatever they put in front of me. For dinner parties like tonight, my favorite chef and restaurateur, Felipé, is on call. Makes life so much easier. Come this way."

We passed a screening room, an office, and a gym with a sauna and went into her bedroom, which also had glass walls with a westward view toward the Pacific Ocean. The wood floors and furniture were a deep brown, darker than I would have expected. Destiny said, "I keep my bedroom dark so I can sleep during the day after late-night recording or on the set."

"But with glass walls, how do you block out the sun?"

Destiny picked up a remote on her nightstand, pressed a button, and suddenly all the windows were completely opaque, and we were plunged into darkness. No light coming through anywhere. "All the walls do this. It's my instant cave." She pressed another button, and light from the recessed fixtures in the ceiling faded up into the room.

"This is incredible! I mean . . . you don't have to worry about curtains or blinds or anything like that."

"Right. Who has time for that?"

"Who lives with you? Your parents?"

"No, my parents are back in Illinois, where I grew up. They live there with my two little brothers."

I was perplexed; she was only sixteen and she lived on her own? "Is that allowed? I mean, you can just live on your own before you're eighteen?

"I'm emancipated, Mango."

"Uh . . . what do you mean?"

"Because of my career, I went to the courts a few years ago to have myself emancipated. That way I can live here, travel whenever necessary, and not have my parents responsible for me or need to be with me. Don't get me wrong, I love my mom and dad and brothers. We have a great relationship, and I go home to visit, and they come here whenever possible. But emancipation makes sense professionally. Max takes care of me like a grandfather. My assistant, Mrs. James, is like a surrogate mom, she lives with me, and I feel safe and secure. Especially with this . . ."

Destiny pressed another button, and a bank of TV monitors rose up from the floor at the foot of the bed. There were high-definition camera surveillance monitors at multiple angles in every room and outdoor area. I could see the Valet Girls waiting for cars to park in front of the house and Dada talking to the chef down in the patio kitchen. Around a fire pit, TJ and his dads were huddled together talking to Max; Tabby and a tall, pale, blonde lady with her hair pulled back in a severe bun were laughing near an infinity pool. I couldn't help it; my mouth hung open, like a dental hygienist was about to clean my teeth. Before I could stop myself, I blurted, "You can afford all of this from working on TV shows?" Oh no, my cheeks got hot as I remembered Mom telling me it was rude to ask people about their salaries, but I just couldn't help myself.

Destiny laughed, "Don't forget, I've been doing this over half my life. TV series, recordings, concerts, sponsorships, personal appearances, modeling contracts, auditioning for parts in movies, which is what I really want to do; I work hard. It's not all glamour and fun, Mango. It takes a lot of discipline. And the rewards are worth it, for the most part, but . . ." She paused, pressed a button, and the wall of monitors sank into the floor and the lighting from above faded. It was completely dark again when she spoke. "When my schedule is clear, and

I get the chance to relax and think about what really matters to me, I do it like this. In the dark. Where no one can see me. Where I can't even see my hand in front of my face. So there is absolutely no judgment. Just me, by myself in my room like when I was a little girl of five or six. Back when my head was full of dreams, and my parents were across the hall just a few steps away."

As the lights faded up and the windows became transparent again, I wondered how I would feel if I were in Destiny's stilettos. I didn't think I'd ever want to be so far away from Mom, Dada, and Jasper. I'd be so lonely. But with a busy schedule like Destiny's, maybe I wouldn't have time to feel lonely. It was strange for someone like me, a regular kid, to feel sorry for a big star like Destiny, but something in me told me she was sad, and I felt sorry for her and a little envious at the same time.

Destiny hopped off the bed. "Hey, why the heck am I being so serious? Let's join the party. Come on!"

The wall slid open, and we stepped onto the balcony and took the stairs down to the patio to join the others. I had no idea that tonight would turn out to be one of the most unexpectedly incredible nights of my life.

CHAPTER EIGHT

Dinner at Eight

S everal new arrivals had joined the party by the time Destiny and I arrived on the patio. She introduced me to her publicist, her yoga instructor, the makeup artist she used exclusively, and her stylist, Voza Clyde, a super-tall, hilarious African American man who had a small film crew following him everywhere to produce a reality show about his life and work with celebrity clients. They asked everyone to sign a waiver agreeing to be on camera for the show. Dada and Max politely refused, and the cameras never pointed in TJ's direction or mine for long.

My head was spinning with all the introductions. I didn't remember any of their names, and I'm pretty sure none of them remembered mine. Destiny was very relaxed and laughed a lot with the people who worked for her, whom she introduced as friends. It made me wonder, *Are people who work for you really your friends? Would they be friends if you didn't pay them? Could you rely on them and confide in them without a business connection?*

Dada was talking to Chef Felipé and his assistants when he waved me over. "This is my daughter, Mango. Her talents are the reason we're out here in Los Angeles."

"Very nice to meet you, Mango. I hope you have great success and enjoy L.A."

"Thank you. The food smells really good."

"I hope it tastes even better. Tonight the menu is all California cuisine. Food cooked with sustainable ingredients that are guided by whatever is available according to the season."

"That's fantastic," Dada said. "In Jamaica we cook that way, too. Our tables are filled with what is fresh, in season, and organic to our culture."

Dada and Chef Felipé fell into a conversation that left space for me to slip away when I saw TJ across the patio looking out at the view. I joined him. "Hey. How's it going?"

"Good. This has been a fun day, huh?"

"Yeah. Full of surprises."

"Like what?"

"Um . . . like the fact that you have two dads."

TJ looked at me, his eyebrows lifted and head tilted curiously. "I don't have two dads."

"You don't? I thought you said Ezra was your dad's husband."

"He is, but he's not my dad. Ezra and my dad are married, but that doesn't make him my dad. I have a great dad who is married to a great guy. I consider Ezra a friend who loves my dad. Just like Mitch is marrying my mother, but I won't consider him a dad—or a friend really. I have one dad. He's great. He's in love with Ezra. It's cool."

"Yeah, I know, but you never mentioned it."

TJ looked at me, a little bemused, innocent, and curious. "Why should I?"

I shrugged, not knowing how to answer. There are things about my family that are different from the majority of families that I don't feel the need to mention. Like that fact that my mother has a prosthetic leg. I don't go around telling everyone I meet about that. The only one I really ever told was Brooklyn, and she used the information to make fun of me. Why should TJ talk about his father's personal life? Ignorant people might use that information to make fun of him. I don't think that was the reason he didn't share the information. I realized he didn't think it was a big deal. He was right, so that's the way I would look at it. It's just a fact and not a big deal.

"Your dad and Ezra both seem really nice," I said. "Did you talk to them about moving out here?"

"No. I won't bring that up until I know if I'm gonna get cast in the show."

"What if you're not cast? Would you still like to live with them?"

TJ took a breath and smiled, "Yeah. I think it's about time I stay close to my dad."

"What about the Halfrican Americans? Is the group breaking up? Have you talked it over with them?"

"No, not yet. Everything's happening so fast. But I'll talk it over with my band when the time comes."

I was about to say, "What about me? You and me?" But I didn't get a chance, because the next thing I knew, there was one of those big, loud whistles you hear when a person does that a thing where they stick two fingers in their mouth and blow. It was loud, piercing, and irritating enough to make everyone turn toward the staircase, and who should be standing there, but . . . Gabriel Faust!

After being startled by the piercing whistle, the party guests turned back to their conversations or whatever they were doing before. It was a stark contrast to how it was when I first met Gabriel Faust. He was practically mobbed by the cast of *Yo, Romeo!* on that first day he showed up at rehearsal. Everyone wanted to get to know him, touch him, take a selfie with him. He was standoffish and reserved behind a huge pair of shades. Now he was trying to draw attention to himself, but it seemed the guests had about as much interest in him as they would a pizza delivery guy.

Gabriel Faust made his way across the room, nodding, smiling, and trying to find a place to fit in. Even Destiny Manaconda was too involved in laughing with her friends to do more than give him a quick hug and peck on the cheek.

He eventually made his way over to TJ and me. "Mango! Teej! *Whoa!* Good to see you again!" I kind of stiffened when he grabbed me up in a hug. I lifted my arms and gently patted his back, holding my breath until he let go. He then did a "bro hug" with TJ, and we all traded strained smiles for a few seconds.

"So? Haven't seen you guys since the show. Man, I'm so bummed that I got sick and couldn't continue. I mean, I had the worst like, uh, strep throat infection. I couldn't even get out of bed."

I squinted at him. "Your manager said you had chicken pox." Busted!

He tried to clean up his mess, but it was still sketchy. "Uh yeah, I did. I mean, everyone thought I did until I saw my doctor and he said it was strep . . . but I kinda broke out all over, too. That was more of a skin thing. Anyway, talk about bad luck, huh?" He had a glaze of sweat over his top lip that he wiped away, "So, how'd the screen test go?"

TJ said, "We haven't done it yet. It's tomorrow."

"Oh, cool! They wanted me to test for a role, but I was like, 'Are you kidding?' Gabriel Faust doesn't test for roles anymore. I mean, c'mon! I'll take a meeting, but I'm beyond testing for roles; know what I'm sayin'?"

I nodded, growing more and more uncomfortable by the second. I didn't want to hold a grudge against Gabriel Faust. I mean, even though his leaving made *Yo, Romeo!* close earlier than planned, things turned out okay for TJ and me. We were at a party in the Hollywood Hills with a bunch of successful people, about to get our shot to be professional actors, too. So, no, I didn't want to judge Gabriel Faust, but I didn't trust him, and how could you become friends with someone you didn't trust?

The tall blonde lady with the severe bun turned out to be Destiny's assistant, Mrs. James. She called for everyone to take seats around a long table; dinner was about to begin. There were place cards telling us where to sit. I was seated across from Dada, next to Destiny, who had placed TJ on her other side. Since Gabriel Faust was an unexpected guest, a chair had to be awkwardly added at the other end of the table next to Mrs. James.

As the food was served, Dada's eyes lit up with each course. First there was California pizza with a thin, light crust. Instead of tomato sauce, it had peanut sauce and was topped with goat cheese and avocado. Dada was impressed with the flavors and texture. Me? Not so much. The second course was cioppino, a seafood stew of squid, Dungeness crab, mussels, clams, and whitefish. It was served in a bowl made of sourdough bread. I loved it. The stew was perfect for an outdoor meal because as the sun went down, the temperature dropped, and the evening was turning quite cool. For dessert there was an amazing chiffon pie made with a shortbread cookie crust filled with a light lemony mousse. I had two servings. TJ had three!

The conversation around all parts of the table was constant and amusing. Destiny, TJ, and I felt like old friends.

Talking and laughing with Destiny was easy and fun. At the other end of the table, Gabriel Faust kept interrupting by banging a spoon on his glass, standing, and making awkward toasts to random guests. Clink-clink-clink on the glass! "Here's to our host, Destiny, my on again, off again, on again, off again tabloid, gossip column girlfriend who keeps my name in the blogs!" Clink-clink-clink on the glass! "A toast to Voza Clyde, the stylist I introduced to Destiny, who now doesn't return my texts! Better get me to sign a release if you want to use this footage on your little reality show!" Clink-clink-clink on the glass! "A toast to my little friends Mango and TJ, all starry-eyed and excited about coming to Hollyweird. The sharks are circling! Watch your backs!" There were uncomfortable smiles around the table. It seemed like Gabriel Faust thought he was being funny, but I felt like he was desperate to be the center of attention.

After dinner, the really Hollywood party part began. We assembled upstairs around the grand piano. Mrs. James played as Destiny sang a new ballad she had just recorded. TJ and I were asked to sing our duet from *Yo, Romeo!* I felt shy, never having sung at a party with so many strangers up close, but after TJ gave me an encouraging wink and nod, I pushed myself to join him. TJ played the piano, and we sang our favorite song from the show, "Duet Forever." Once we started, I connected with TJ, and all my nervousness went away.

I think Gabriel Faust felt some kind of way because he wasn't asked to sing. He actually got up and went to the restroom during our song. When he came back, he sat down at the piano and sang a song he said was going to be on his next album, called "Trippin' on Sunset." It was about driving fast cars and picking up girls. Cute.

Destiny asked if anyone else wanted to perform. I was shocked when TJ stood and raised his hand. "I want to sing a song I wrote for my dad. We, uh, haven't spent time together in a while and since there's no piano at his house and I didn't bring my guitar to L.A., this is my chance." Everyone applauded, encouraging him to do it. His father and Ezra looked surprised as TJ sat at the piano and sang a beautiful ballad called, "Love How You Love." It was a heartfelt song about how loving was always right, and everyone had the right to love. I watched Mr. Malachi as TJ was singing and saw his eyes get moist with appreciation. Gabriel Faust was sitting close to the piano, obviously paying more attention to his phone than TJ or the song. I thought he was being rude. I guess it's kind of hard getting used to not being the center of attention when you've been catered to and gushed over most of your life.

Around ten o'clock, Max suggested that TJ and I leave so we could get a good night's sleep and be rested for our screen tests in the morning. We said our goodbyes and thanked Destiny for inviting us to her party. I asked, "Will you be at our screen test tomorrow?"

"I wanted to. In fact, I was planning on testing with you, but . . ." She leaned in close. "This is totally between us, Davesh Muhammad Poitrine, you know, the fabulous French film director, has asked me to have a Face2Face 'dinner' meeting with him tomorrow. It'll be nine in the morning here, but six in the evening in Paris, so . . . I'll have to be here, all dressed and glammed to impress him. It's not every day an American TV actor like me gets to meet a genius like Davesh Muhammad Poitrine."

I gasped. "Wasn't his last movie nominated for a bunch of Academy Awards?"

"Yes! *Bitter Croissant*; it was amazing! Did you see it?"

"Uh, no, but I heard about it."

"It's beyond! Anyway, I sent in a self tape auditioning for his next film months ago, and now . . ." She leaned in closer. "Please keep this between us. My biggest dream is to be in movies. Great movies. Playing real, complex characters. Not like this TV fluff."

TV fluff? *TV fluff* had given her this great Hollywood Hills life. I thought she sounded a tad ungrateful, but I couldn't judge her. I hadn't walked in her shoes. I didn't share her dreams. Maybe I'd feel the same way if I'd experienced the years of hard work Destiny had put in. As we headed up the stairs, Destiny returned to her party, calling over her shoulder, "Break a leg, you two! I'm rooting for ya!"

Outside, while Dada, Tabby, and I were waiting for the Valet Girls to bring the van, and TJ, his dad, and Ezra were waiting for their Tesla, Gabriel Faust came out of the house. There was a shiny, sleek, mustard-yellow Maserati parked right outside. Gabriel Faust walked over to it, saying, "Some cars are too high-end to risk a Val Lady scratching it up." He laughed at his little joke as he revved up his vehicle and tore off, sending clouds of dust and a spray of pebbles behind. We could hear his tires squealing as he sped around the curves on the way down the hill.

All of a sudden, my eyelids were drooping, and I couldn't stop yawning. TJ was behaving the same way. I said, "What's wrong with me, it's only a little after ten."

Mr. Malachi said, "It's a little after ten here, but it's after one a.m. on the East Coast, where you all come from."

That's right. I hadn't realized there was a three-hour time difference between here and home. I'd been up before sunrise when we left for the airport. It seemed like so long ago. So much had happened in one day. I leaned on Dada. He put an arm around me. I closed my eyes, eager to crawl into bed and sleep more deeply than I'd ever slept before. I really needed the rest, because tomorrow would be a day that decided a big part of my future.

CHAPTER NINE

Holding Pattern

I slept so hard on the drive back to the hotel that I barely remember Dada carrying me up to my room, where I just kicked off my shoes and climbed into bed. Then the dreams began. . . .

I was running down the hill on Sunset Plaza Drive where Destiny lived, being chased by Gabriel Faust's Maserati. He was driving, but the grill on the car was opening its "mouth" and laughing. Not a jolly laugh, but a maniacal *I'm gonna get you* laugh. The next thing I knew, I was in a pool that was as big as an ocean. Symphony and Kashara rose up from the waves as a kind of mermaid creature with two bodies that shared one tail, which they kept slamming on the water to splash me. I swam away from them really fast, but they would dive underwater and then emerge right in front of me, trying to force me to eat garlic chicken! Next I was at the studio on the soundstage. It was time for my audition, and TJ kept telling me to hurry up to the set, but my teeth kept crumbling and falling out along the way. By the time I got in front of the cameras, I was toothless. I was trying to say my lines without opening my mouth, but no one could understand what I was saying!

I woke up in a sweat and quickly ran my tongue over my teeth—thankfully, they were still there. What a relief! I checked my phone. It was a little before five. I should have gone back to sleep, but I was afraid. What if I had another horrible dream? Dada was snoring softly in his room, so I went into the living room, took out my script, and went over my screen test lines.

It was difficult to concentrate, because my mind kept wandering back to Destiny's dinner party and all the people I'd met. I was trying to imagine myself in Destiny's place. What if I lived I a house like that with my assistant? My family would still be back home, and I'd be emancipated, legally on my own. Would I like that? Would I be happy on the outside and sad on the inside? Maybe Mom could be my assistant and Dada could be my personal chef? Then we could live together. But would things be different if I paid them? Would it feel like they were my parents or my employees? Would I miss my friends at Trueheart Middle School? Would Izzy, Hailey Joanne, and the dramanerds forget all about me?

Before I knew it, Dada was gently shaking me awake on the couch. I didn't feel rested at all. Instead of nightmares, this time I'd had anxiety sleep filled with endless questions I couldn't answer. It was seven o'clock, time to get ready for my screen test. We also had to pack our bags for the flight home.

At the breakfast buffet in the hotel lobby, Dada served me a plate of scrambled eggs, turkey sausage, a blueberry muffin, and cantaloupe. All things I like, but I couldn't eat. Symphony, Kashara, and their mothers were across the room, whispering and throwing hard, cold shade in my direction. At least, that's how I felt as I kept my tongue busy, checking for any loose teeth.

TJ was already in the van when Tabby picked up Dada and me. I slid into the seat next to him. We were just about to pull off when Symphony and her mother appeared on the curb, waving frantically. Tabby stopped, and they climbed aboard. Tabby looked at his schedule and said, "I wasn't supposed to pick you up for your callback until this afternoon at three."

Symphony said, "We know, but I just wanted to get to the studio early, so I can relax"—her eyes slid over to me—"and observe." She squeezed in next to me, smiled, reached her hand across me to TJ, and said, "Hey there! I'm Symphony Burns."

TJ shook her hand and said, "Hi, I'm TJ."

Still holding on to his hand, Symphony said, "TJ? That's nice. What are you testing for?"

"Uh . . . the Destiny Manaconda project."

"*Ooooh*, me too! I mean, I have a callback today."

I squirmed, to remind her that her arm was across my stomach, but she continued to ignore me, holding on to TJ's hand with a kung fu grip.

"I bet you'll get cast, with those green eyes of yours, they'll look amazing in hi-def."

I couldn't believe it! She was flirting with TJ right in front of me. My TJ! Of course, she didn't know he was *my TJ*. I mean . . . he really wasn't mine, except as a friend. But in any case, how dare she! TJ kind of blushed and wrenched his hand out of hers. I took her forearm away from my stomach and placed it in her lap.

"Oh, I'm so sorry, Marlo. Was I being rude?"

"It's Mango."

"Oh, that's right, like the fruit. Pardon me. So, your test is this morning, huh? Are you prepared? Need any help?"

I sighed and gritted my teeth, answering her three rapid-fire questions, "Yes. Yes, and no, thank you."

"All right. Excuse me, I'm going to sit with mother and do some relaxation breathing exercises. Nice meeting you TJ. Good luck, Mango. I'll be watching!"

Watching? Judging is more like it. *OMGZ*, if I wasn't nervous before, I was super-nervous and self-conscious now.

The rest of the morning was distorted and blurry. All I know is my stomach was in knots, and I had so much trouble concentrating. When Dionne, who was directing the test, spoke to me, it seemed like her voice was in an echo chamber a thousand miles away. I couldn't keep my attention focused on her, not with all the people on the crew, about fifty men and women, hot lights, and an overhead boom microphone all focused on me. I knew somewhere, hidden on the soundstage in the dark behind all of this, Symphony was watching and probably laughing at how incompetent I was. This was torture, and I couldn't wait for it to end!

Tabby dropped us off at the airport before noon. TJ, who seemed completely relaxed and pleased with his screen test, was staying behind to spend time with his dad. Dada and I had a couple of hours to wait before our flight. We shopped for books and magazines to read on the plane, overpriced "Los Angeles" T-shirts, key chains, and other souvenirs for Mom, Jasper, and my friends back home (I even found a fill-in-the-blank Hollywood Walk of Fame star for Izzy!).

Dada was trying to act upbeat and encouraging, but nothing he did—not the corny jokes, silly faces, or cajoling could break through the wall of failure I was building, brick by brick, as I replayed my awful screen test. Still, I appreciated how protective and tender he was about my feelings. He was making sure I had the space I needed to "lick my wounds" and take care of myself.

I had never failed at anything so badly before. A year earlier, I had auditioned, under duress, the first time and had won the lead role. I later played the role again in New York City and had gotten great reviews. Now, here I was in

Hollywood, testing for the biggest opportunity of my life, and I had risen to the occasion like roadkill. I really stunk up the studio.

We finally boarded the plane and took our first-class seats, which I no longer felt I deserved. I wrapped myself in the blanket the flight attendant offered (even though Hailey Joanne had warned me against using the "cootie-filled wrappers"), turned toward the window away from Dada, and pretended to sleep. Still, my mind was racing. I never, ever wanted to think about or go back to Hollywood again. I had let everyone down: Maxwell Paige, Destiny, TJ, Dada, Mom, . . . everyone who believed in me. I just wanted to go home and forget the whole experience. Even though I knew Izzy, Hailey Joanne, and my dramanerds friends would want to hear every last detail, I wouldn't say a word.

I decided I would pretend to be sick. I would make believe I was so sick that everyone would feel sorry for me and, after a week or two, forget that I ever had a screen test. But what kind of sickness? It couldn't be something so horrific that Dada and Mom would make me see a doctor who could prove I was faking. I had to come up with something they couldn't detect with an X-ray or blood test. I decided to pretend I had a massive headache. One of those migraines. I'd seen movies where people with migraines had to stay in darkened rooms and have complete quiet for days on end. Yes, that was my way out! Not only would I keep my friends away and the need to talk about my ordeal, if I was truly convincing, I could prove to myself that I was still a good actor, even after my screen test disaster.

The pilot made an announcement about flying speed and altitude and how long it would take to get back east. The flight attendants did their routine about seat belts and what to do if the cabin pressure plummeted and oxygen masks fell from the console above. The lights in the cabin were dimmed. The flight attendants buckled themselves into their seats. The engines revved. I was on my way home.

Then, suddenly, the engines wound down until there was only a low hum again. Cabin lights came back on. The flight attendant unbuckled and answered a dinging intercom. Something was up.

I peered out from my blanket cocoon as the flight attendant reopened the door to the cabin. I asked Dada, "What's going on?"

Dada shrugged. "Maybe some movie star or politician is late for the flight."

The desk attendant who had checked our tickets before boarding hurried onto the plane, briskly scoped first class, and headed directly toward Dada and me. She said, "Mr. and Miss Fuller, gather your things and come with me, please."

CHAPTER TEN

Holding Pattern, Part Two

As we rolled our suitcases past the pool on our way back to the lobby of the Valley Arms, I could feel the eyes of the other guests upon us. Two guests in particular, whom I believe imagined they'd seen the last of me. They watched from the pool, mouths hanging open as I gave them a slight glance and the most Mona Lisa mysterious smile I could come up with.

What I was doing checking back into the hotel was pretty much a mystery to me, too. After stepping off the jetway and back inside LAX, we found Maxwell Paige there, waiting for us.

"Thank goodness I caught you before takeoff."

Dada said, "What's going on, Max?"

"Just a minute." Max turned to the desk attendant, "You can continue the flight now—"

Dada interrupted, holding his hand out to the flight attendant. "Hold on. We're supposed to be on that flight home. My wife's expecting us."

"Please, Sid, trust me; you'll want to stay."

68

"Why? I'm sorry, but Mango's had a rough day out here, and we're going home!" Dada turned toward the attendant about to close the jetway door. Max reached for Dada's arm as we were turning to leave. Dada shook his hand off. That's when I got a little nervous. I'd never seen Dada like this before. I stepped between them and said, "Max do you need us to stay for something good or something bad?"

Max smiled down at me. "Why would I ever want you to stay for something bad, Mango? As your manager, I'll be your champion."

I looked at Dada. "We could get another flight if we miss this one."

"And if we can't get one today," Dada asked, "when your mom and Jasper are expecting us?"

"I'll get the studio to send you home on a private jet," Max offered, "even if I have to pay out of my own pocket. Please, Sid, let the plane go, so we can talk."

Dada thought for a second and nodded, releasing the flight.

We walked back a ways through the terminal and took seats at a JoJo Juice stand. I ordered a mango smoothie, of course. Max had a pineapple and plum, and Dada refused to drink anything; how could he, with his arms folded firmly across his chest?

Max started, "I know this is last minute, believe me. I expected you to be upset by my stopping the plane the way I did, but an opportunity may be opening up for Mango, and I don't want her to miss it."

"But I was horrible," I said. "I can tell when I mess up, and that's what I did all morning."

"Okay. I'll be straight with you, the screen test was pretty much a complete washout. But that's not the only thing that goes into making a decision, and right now . . . Let me put it this way, big decisions are being made, and I have a gut feeling you need to be out here."

"A gut feeling?" Dada's arms finally loosened and his hands gripped the edge of the table. "You pulled us off the plane for a *gut feeling*? Nothing concrete! Just a feeling? You've got to be kidding me!"

"Sid, that's how I operate. I've created stars and built my business on my gut. I believe in your daughter, and things are happening as we speak—"

"What kind of things? What?"

Max rubbed his chin with his long slender fingers and sat back. "I'm sorry, Sid, and you, too, Mango, but I just can't divulge what's going on just yet."

Dada slapped the table with his palm. "Oh, great! What am I supposed to tell my wife, huh? We're not coming home but I can't tell you why, because I don't know why."

"Tell her we need a few more days with Mango on the Coast to see how things shake out, and in the meantime while you wait, I'll send you and Mango on a VIP tour of Los Angeles. I'm talking priority tours of Disneyland, Universal Studios, Knott's Berry Farm, Legoland, the works!"

"Margie don't care about none of that."

"She might," I said, putting my palm on top of Dada's hand. "I mean, she might care about it if she and Jasper could fly out and join us." I turned to Max. "Do you think you could make that happen, Max?"

Max's smile was so broad, it looked like his teeth were giving me a standing ovation. "The minute your mother says yes, they're as good as on a flight."

That's how I, Mango Delight Fuller, saved the day, and we wound up back at the Valley Arms.

Convincing Mom was not as simple as I'd imagined. In the Uber back to the hotel, Dada made a quick call to let her in on the fact that we would not be arriving home right away. The questions came out rapid fire, like a baseball batting cage machine run amuck. But Dada convinced her to hold off until we got back to the Valley Arms, where we could discuss everything over a Face2Face.

I was pacing back and forth, and Dada was on the couch when Mom connected and immediately launched into questions, "What happened? What's going on? Sid, how am I supposed to just jump up and fly away to La-La Land? Huh? I didn't plan on any of this."

"Neither did I, sweetheart, but things happen pretty fast out here."

"How do you know? You don't even know what's happening. How do you know whether it'll be fast or not?"

"Margie, please, stop asking me questions I can't answer!"

"Didn't you say Mango's screen test was awful? Why would they want to keep her there if—"

"Margie!" Dada interrupted Mom. "Mango is sitting right here. She can hear you."

I moved over to the couch next to Dada and waved. "Hi, Mom."

If Mom had been a building, the expression on her face would have looked like someone had detonated a demolition bomb, and it crumpled seven floors to the ground.

"Oh, hi, honey. Um . . . I didn't mean anything by what I just said. I mean, Dada didn't actually say that . . . uh, he, um, inferred it was not, you know, great."

I laughed. It was rare to see Marjorie Fuller at a loss for words and backtracking like a car in reverse without a rearview mirror. "It's okay, Mom. I really laid an egg at the studio today. I know that. In fact, everybody on the crew and probably everyone here at the hotel knows it, too, because a certain sour Symphony down at the pool definitely spread the word. I'm okay."

"You sure, baby?"

"Yes, I'm fine, and I don't know what's going on, but wouldn't it be fun if we were all together touring L.A. and having a blast? Do you know how great it'd be for Jasper to meet Mickey and Donald and his favorite, Goofy?"

Mom smiled and sank back on the sofa in our living room back home. She took a minute to slow her breathing, and it seemed as though I could see the synapses in her brain

72

sparking. "Well, I do have a few vacation days I can use. Target won't collapse without me."

"Are you sure, honey?" asked Dada.

"No, I'm not sure, but I'd be a pitiful fool to pass up a free trip to Los Angeles. You know, I've never even seen the Pacific Ocean?"

Dada and I high-fived each other. "That's great, baby. We can't wait for you to get here."

"It may take a couple of days. I have to pack and make arrangements at work and—"

I broke in. "Don't worry, you're going to have help. Max's assistant, Jericka, is flying to you to help pack and everything. She's even going to be on the flight with you to help take care of Jasper. It's all set, Mom; you're leaving tomorrow afternoon, and we're going to have the best vacation we've ever had."

Dada put his arm around my shoulder. "Actually, Mango-gal, this is going to be the first *real* vacation we've ever had as a family. And you know what?"

"What?"

"It's all because of you." He kissed my cheek, and I beamed a glow as bright as a supernova.

CHAPTER ELEVEN

Tip the Pot and Serve the Tea

The next day, we decided to hang out at the hotel pool while we waited for Mom and Jasper to arrive. Max arranged for Felipé, Destiny's favorite personal chef, to take us on a restaurant tour to sample more Cali Cuisine later that evening. I have to say, Max really was working overtime to make us feel comfortable, entertained, and important—especially Dada. I was sure Max knew he'd have to impress both of my parents before they'd agree to my signing a management contract with him and a performing contract with Chrysalis Studio that could change my family's way of life.

I woke up around six in the morning and couldn't get back to sleep, so I immediately called Izzy to fill her in on all that was going on. I knew she'd be awake, because it was after nine in the morning, East Coast time. When I told her how badly the screen test had gone, Izzy said, "Did you sing for them? There's no way it could be as bad as you say if you sang for them."

"I didn't have to sing. My character was going to be a backup singer to Destiny, so my singing really didn't matter."

"Girl, that's ridiculous! You sing better than Destiny. Better than anyone I know . . . except me, of course."

"Of course!"

"Oh, please, you're just saying that because I said that first."

"Okay. You're right!"

She hooted, "Mango!" We laughed and went back and forth about how much we admired each other's singing and how much we missed each other. We also spent a good deal of time making plans to take Trueheart Middle School by storm during our upcoming sophomore year.

Next, I called Hailey Joanne, who'd just returned from her riding lessons and couldn't stop talking about her new horse, Hervé. She had named the young stallion after the French boy she'd met in Paris and was still crushing on. "L'amour, l'amour tous les jours, l'amour every day!" she gushed.

As soon as I could get a word in, I told her about our family's lucky "free vacation." Hailey Joanne proceeded to fill me in on all the best rides and attractions I should definitely not miss. I took notes, because she'd already been everywhere we were planning to go more than once.

Hailey Joanne really got interested when I told her about Kashara and Symphony. "Don't trust them," she warned. "I knew girls exactly like that when I spent fourth and fifth grade in a Swiss boarding school, Our Lady of Salt Tears. I had to threaten to jump off the Matterhorn to make my parents bring me back the home to the United States. Those girls used to get together in the dark caverns under the school and burn my name in cauldrons to make my complexion pop out in pimples!"

"Hailey Joanne, I don't think these girls are that bad."

"Trust me, watch your back and use a moisturizing, antibacterial bar soap morning, noon, and night!"

Around nine, I thought it'd be safe to call TJ and fill him in on all that happened. I shouldn't have been surprised when he told me he'd been awake since six o'clock, too. We were both still on East Coast time.

He was also too shocked to disguise his surprise. When I told him I was still in L.A., he said, "Seriously? You're kidding me! They wanted *you* to stay after your screen test?"

"Don't hold back about how bad you think I was," I said, not truly mad, because I appreciated his honesty.

"Oh man, sorry, but for real, I'm glad you're still here. My dad, Ezra, and I are driving down to Malibu today. Wanna come? They belong to a beach club out there. It's supposed to be really swanky."

"Swanky? Where'd you come up with that word, *A Gentlemen's Guide to Society Slang*?"

TJ laughed, but I could feel him blushing over the phone. The thought of a spending a day with him by the ocean at a "swanky" beach club was tempting, but I wanted to hang out with Dada today. Besides, we needed to rest up for our tour of L.A. I told TJ about it, and he was excited about Disney and

Universal Studios. He'd been there before with his dad on visits out west, but Mr. Malachi was tired of having to go to amusement parks every time TJ or some other relative from back east visited. I asked if he'd like to come along with us. TJ said, "Yeah! It'll be crispy seeing those places with someone whose never been there before." I promised to fill him in as soon as the plans were set.

I was getting sleepy again when Dada came to my room, ready to go downstairs for breakfast. I finally had an appetite and polished off two pieces of thick French toast, a couple of turkey sausages, a fried egg, and a blueberry yogurt! Dada and I got into our swimsuits, put on sunscreen, found a couple of deck chairs by the pool, and lay out in the sun. After waking before dawn and wolfing down a big breakfast, I could barely keep my eyes open. The California sun felt amazing and turned my closed eyelids a dreamy shade of burnt orange. Seriously thinking about needing to buy a pair of sunglasses, I fell into a deep, dreamless sleep.

I was awakened about thirty minutes later by high-pitched "Hey, girl!" and "Mango, are you going to sleep the day away, sis?" I cranked my eyes open. The sun was eclipsed by Symphony's broad-brimmed hat and Kashara's one-hundred-watt smile. I lifted myself up on my elbows and checked—Dada wasn't in is chair next to me.

"Where's my father?"

Kashara pointed to the pool. "He's out there doing the breaststroke and giving our mothers heatstroke."

Symphony nodded. "He sure is handsome. My mother thinks he could be an actor or a leading man."

My brow furrowed. "My mother feels the same, and she'll be here first thing tomorrow morning."

The girls looked at each other with a quick *well, so much for that* pout, then turned their laser focus back to me.

"*Sooooo*, how was dinner with Destiny last night? I heard Gabriel Faust and Voza Clyde were there."

"Yes, they were there." They sighed, and the rapid-fire questions began.

"Were Voza and his husband filming their reality show about being stylists to the stars?"

"Are you going to be on it?"

"What about Gabriel Faust? Is he still a dream?"

"Oh, Symphony, please! His dream turned into a nightmare years ago."

"Yeah, it's such a shame, being washed up at such a young age."

I had to get away. "I need to jump in the pool and cool off. Be right back." I bolted out of the deck chair with no intention of being right back and slid into the water. Dada was doing laps back and forth across the width of the pool. I joined him, determined to stay in water long enough to prune, in order to avoid the "sisters" and their interrogation.

Dada gave me some diving lessons. Not on the diving board—I was not ready for that just yet—but from the side of the pool. He gave me a lot of tips on how to hold my arms up, keep my legs straight, and have my feet pointed. I felt Kashara and Symphony watching, but I ignored them and put all my concentration on Dada.

After lunch we went back to our room. Dada was flipping through a couple of gourmet magazines. I was settling down to read Jacqueline Woodson's *Another Brooklyn*. She was one of my favorite authors, so I'd picked it up at the airport, intending to dive into it on the plane ride home, but that didn't happen. I was just settling into the first chapter when there was a barrage of knocking at the door.

Symphony and Kashara burst in before I could get the door opened all the way. "Girl, we have to talk," Kashara said. "We've got bad news."

"Real bad," Symphony said. "Not just bad for you, but for us, too."

"That makes it doubly-triply bad!" Kashara took me by the arm and led me to *my* room. How did she know which room was mine? I'll never know, but as soon as we got there she said, "Sit down. You're gonna need to be seated when you here this. Guess what?"

"Hold on, Kashara, I should be the one to break it to her!"

"Why come?"

"Because why, I'm the one who had the callback, so it hurts me more than you since you only had one audition."

"Excuse me, Miss It Don't Matter If You Get A Call Back, Only How Well You Did!"

"You know, that's how I feel, but still, my heart is way more broken than yours, sis."

Kashara flipped her box braids, plopped down the bed next to me, and said, "Go on, tip the pot and serve the tea, if you insist."

Symphony removed her floppy wide-brimmed hat, smoothed down the auburn cowlick that always seemed to pop up whenever she removed her hat, and said, "Destiny Manaconda's been fired! Her show has been canceled. Might is well repack your bags and go home!"

CHAPTER TWELVE

Gastronomical

We met Felipé at his restaurant, Chaos, which was just across the street from the Grove, a popular outdoor L.A. shopping mall that featured an elegant fountain with water that danced to music. Again, I wore the one dress Mom had made me pack. I was so grateful to have it with me. Felipé greeted us like royalty. "Welcome, my friends! So happy to see you again. I've prepared a very special tasting menu just for you." We followed him into a dining room just off the kitchen. This was the "chef's table," a space reserved for honored guests. Dada and Felipé were deep into chefs' talk when small bites of delicacies that weren't even on the menu arrived at our table one by one.

Once again, my appetite was playing hide and seek, because my thoughts were consumed with Kashara and Symphony's news. *Had Destiny really been fired from the show? Was it all over? Had Dionne Harmony's dream of creating her own television series been crushed? Did any part of what was happening have anything to do with me and why I was still in L.A.? How? Why?*

I didn't say anything to Dada about what was troubling me. I wanted him to have fun and enjoy the culinary tour we were on tonight. Instead, I tried calling Max, but my calls went straight to voicemail. I tried googling Destiny to see if there was any news in the gossip blogs, but I came up with nothing.

I remembered Destiny telling me about her meeting with the French movie director. Did whatever was going on have something to do with that? Of course, I didn't mention any of what Destiny told me to Symphony and Kashara. They would've had a field day with information like that. I didn't even tell them I knew Gabriel Faust from my summer in New York. I wasn't trying to keep it a secret from them, but I was afraid they'd never stop pumping me for information and dirt if they knew.

After about ten assorted amuse-bouches, which were delicious but I only nibbled because of my worries, we set off on a tour of the many different types of food L.A. had to offer. Felipé drove us in his Tesla, which was so new it still had that awesome new car smell. As Dada settled into the passenger seat, he said, "Bruh, this car is sweet! I get the feeling a chef can do very well out here in L.A!"

"You're right about that. If you have a special talent to offer and get a chance to show what you've got, the sky's the limit. Take your daughter, Mango, for example. She's about to become the next big thing."

"Really?" Dada said. "Do you know something we don't know?"

Felipé smiled and shrugged. "It's a vibe, man, a vibe. You can feel it in the air when someone is about to break big."

Dada turned, looked at me in the back seat, and smiled. There was a twinkle in his eyes, an excitement like mini-fireworks in his pupils. Unfortunately, his excitement didn't translate directly to me. Somehow the "vibe" Felipé was talking about triggered the mango pit in my stomach, and it grew heavier and heavier all through the rest of the culinary tour, as I wondered and worried about what the future held for me.

All my worries blew away the second Mom and Jasper arrived at LAX the next morning. Jasper ran straight to me. I knelt to hug him, and he almost knocked me over as he threw his arms around my neck shouting, "Mango! Mango! I miss you!" My eyes grew wet. Even though I'd only been gone about three days, I thought he seemed so much bigger than when I left. I wanted to squeeze him and freeze the moment in time.

My baby brother wasn't really a baby anymore. He'd reached a whole new level of personhood, and I'd missed seeing it happen because of how much I'd been away from home over the summer. Having my family together again, all at once I knew that, no matter what, I needed to be with them all the time. I was not the kind of girl who could be emancipated from her parents like Destiny. I wanted to be with them. Whatever came my way, I'd have to make sure we stayed together.

Mom hugged me tight, and I indulged I the coconut scent of her locs. All the people in the crowded arrivals terminal seem to disappear at our reunion. All except one. There was a very pretty young lady with large eyes and a cute pixie haircut standing nearby. She was holding on to the cart that held Mom's and Jasper's suitcases and his car seat. She smiled a smile that was somehow familiar. I moved toward her and said, "Hi, I'm Mango."

"Hi. Nice to meet you. I'm Jericka Paige."

"Paige? Are you related to Max?"

Mom jumped in. "She's his daughter! I'mma tell you, I would never have made it here without her. Jericka is a miracle worker, and I'm never letting her go!" We laughed, and introductions were made all around as we headed for the curb where Tabby waited with the van.

Jericka sat next to me on the ride back to the Valley Arms. She told me all about graduating from law school the previous spring. Her specialty was entertainment law (I never knew there was such a thing; I guess it's because they didn't need that kind of attorney on shows like *Law and Order*). "My goal is to be a manager like my dad. He wants me to learn the business from the bottom up. I've cleaned his offices, hand-washed his cars, worked in the mail room, made deliveries, handled his schedule, anything you can think of, so I'll be ready to take charge when he retires."

The idea of Max retiring just when we were seeing if he'd represent me made me anxious. "Is he planning on retiring soon?"

"Are you kidding? I'll probably be his age and still have to pry the keys to the office from his fingers." She laughed. "Anyway, I'm here for you and your family. This is one of the biggest responsibilities he's given me so far, and I want to make good. So I'm completely at your disposal. Anything you need, all you have to do is ask."

I took the opportunity to ask her if the rumors about Destiny being fired from her show were true. Jericka smiled and shook her head. "The rumors out here are crazy. Did you ever play the telephone game? The one where one person whispers a phrase in the ear of the person next to them, and then that person does the same thing, all around the circle until the last person in the line recites the phrase, which has changed so completely by that time, it's unrecognizable?"

"Yeah, we used to play that at camp when I was a kid."

"Well, that's what happens here in Hollywood all the time. Destiny has definitely not been fired, but that's all I can say at this point. Just be patient, and all will be revealed."

I had the feeling Jericka had just told me to mind my own business in the most friendly way possible. So, I decided to put thoughts of Destiny and my fate on pause and just enjoy my free time. For the next three days, Jericka planned and coordinated trips to Disneyland, where Jasper was awestruck by all that Magic Kingdom had to offer, and Universal Studios, where it was my turn to be astounded by the rides and a visit to Hogwarts before the ride opened to the public for the day. Even TJ, who had been to all the attractions more than once, was knocked out by the fact that we never had to stand in any lines. In fact, we were driven everywhere in tricked-out golf carts. Although Mom never complained, I'm sure she was grateful not to have to be up on her prosthetic leg all day.

On the third day we got a super surprise. Jericka moved us all to the Windsong, an elegant resort hotel right on the beach at Santa Monica. It was a dream come true for Mom, as she finally got a chance to see the Pacific Ocean. But when she finally stepped into the water, Mom cried out, "Oh my gosh, this water is freezing! Get me out of here!" And she refused to go back into the ocean again.

TJ, his dad, and Ezra joined us for a sunset picnic in a cabana on the beach. It was the perfect end to a the most lovely day ever. I'd never seen Mom so relaxed and . . . I guess the word is *charming*. My mother is kind and loving, but there was always something "on guard" about her that seemed to completely disappear that day. She laughed and joked without the sarcasm or edge that usually added a sting to her sense of humor. As the sun went down and the sky above the horizon went from orange to lavender to navy blue, I wondered about the magic California seemed to be casting on both my parents. My hunger to find a way to stay here was reignited. What wouldn't I do to keep the warmth of this glow on my family?

When the waiters and hotel staff arrived to clear away the meal and cabana, Max was with them. Seeing Jericka standing next to her father, you could immediately see how his handsome face had become beautiful when his daughter inherited his features. Dada joked, "Jericka must look like her mama, because she surely don't take after you, Max!" They volleyed pleasantly back and forth about whom Jericka and I received our "shine" from. It was embarrassing but also warm and funny.

Before TJ and his dad and Ezra departed, Max made an announcement. "Destiny has a big concert ending her summer tour tomorrow night at the Hollywood Bowl, and you all are invited as VIP guests. You'll practically be seated on the stage!"

That was a great surprise, but I hadn't packed anything to go to an event like that. The Hollywood Bowl was a historic venue, and all I had to wear was the one dress Mom had forced me to pack for the trip. Maybe Max could read the worry on my face, because the next thing out of his mouth was "TJ, Mango, and family, Jericka has arranged to bring you an assortment of designer outfits to choose among, if you desire. In addition, you will all be treated to an exclusive spa day here at the Windsong—at your convenience, of course."

Whoa! This was uber-crisp. Having designer outfits bought to our room and exclusive spa treatments? This was a Hailey Joanne type of lifestyle that I was not accustomed to! We all cheered, and Mom and Dada even did a little dance on the way back to the hotel.

That Maxwell Paige, he really was rolling out the red carpet for all of us. He and I shared a smile as everyone else celebrated. He was up to something. I had a feeling this was the frosting being whipped up for a master plan cake that he was already baking. But what kind of cake could it be, red velvet or devil's food?

CHAPTER THIRTEEN

Starry, Starry Night

The suite at the Windsong was uber-plush! Two large bedrooms, each with their own bathroom, a kitchenette, a dining area, a living room big enough for three couches and a sliding glass door that led to a private patio. Mom couldn't get over how elegant and stylish everything was. She said, "I feel like I'm in a movie, and Tom Cruise or Idris Elba is going to walk through the door at any minute!" I was kind of puzzled by her fantasy movie idol choices but, hey, she was a product of her generation.

After putting Jasper to bed, Mom, Dada, and I stayed up into the wee hours of the morning trying to find a way to help Mom beat jet lag. We didn't want her to get sleepy during Destiny's concert tomorrow night. At first we played twenty-one blackjack. I won so many hands, I think my parents got a little discouraged. Haha! Later we sat around thinking out loud about what it might be like to move to L.A.

"There are plenty of Target stores here in Los Angeles," Mom said. "It probably wouldn't be too difficult for me to transfer and keep my position as a manager."

"Los Angeles is right up there with New York and London when it comes to restaurants and culinary opportunities," Dada said. "In fact, I already got a nibble."

"Nibble?" I sat up. "What kind of nibble?"

"Every other month, Felipé holds a guest chef night at Chaos. He offered me the chance to do a chef night if we stay in L.A. long enough for him to publicize it." Dada went on and on about the dishes he would create to showcase his skills. "With all the fresh seafood and veggies I can find out here, there's no limit to the ways I could dazzle his clientele."

We were all so caught up in California dreams, we each fell asleep right there in the living room, on our very own couches.

Of course, Jasper woke around seven in the morning, but the amazing Jericka showed up just in time. She got him fed and dressed and took him on an outing to the beach, complete with a red plastic bucket and sand tools. She was every drop of miraculous. Mom, Dada, and I found our way to our beds and slept until noon.

After we finished brunch, lounging on our private patio, estheticians arrived for our spa treatments. Facials, massages, and mani-pedis without having to leave our rooms! Mom, Dada, and I were taking "groupie" selfies in our seaweed-avocado face masks when Jericka arrived with Jasper. He burst out crying at the sight of the three of us. It was so funny, poor little thing. Mom had to remove her mask early to get him to calm down.

It was a little after three, and Mom, Dada, Jasper, and I were sitting around in luxurious white terry cloth bath-robes when the door chimes rang. I opened the door and was stunned to find Voza Clyde. "Hello, my little fabulous superstar! Mango, right? Didn't we meet the other night at Destiny's? Yes, I remember, your handsome father wouldn't agree to your being on camera. Too bad! My show is going to break the international web. How could it not—I'm Voza!"

Mom came to the door. "What's going on?"

"You, diva, you're what's going on! Voza is about to find your fabulous and turn up the heat! *Yasssss!*"

Mom and Dada's eyes were bulging as Voza strode into the suite followed by his assistants, three racks of designer clothes, shoes, and accessories. "Chose whatever you like, then Voza will make better choices, and my little minions will make any alterations necessary maximize your fab! Just remember, when the night is over, everything goes back to my designer friends who sent their best casual couture, because Voza is irresistible. You can feel it, can't you? Voza KNOWS you can feel the heat!"

From the way I was blushing, I definitely could feel Voza's heat and see why he was considered irresistible, but why me? Why us? I had to ask. "Mr. Clyde . . . ?"

"Voza, diva. I only answer to Voza or Your Imperial Highness."

"Sorry, Voza. I just have to ask, why are you doing all this for us?"

"Maxwell, of course. He's my manager. Max made me a star, honey. His wish is my command. Now come on, y'all, let's get fabulous!"

Voza dressed us in casual chic attire. All one-of-a-kind pieces that were nothing like we'd ever worn before. Destiny's glam squad stopped by before they had to prepare her for the concert and did our hair and makeup. Mom's locs never looked fresher, but she was extremely uncomfortable getting her makeup done. "I couldn't stop sweating! I never had anybody up so close touching my face before! Never again. I'm serious. I'm just fine with the eyelashes I was born with; these things got me blinking fast as hummingbird wings!"

Dada and I laughed and reassured Mom that she looked gorgeous. Tabby was waiting for us outside the hotel, but there was no van this time; instead there was a luxury party bus! TJ, his dad, and Ezra were inside, along with Kashara and Symphony. I had asked Jericka if they could come along because I knew how much they loved Destiny Manaconda, and I thought this way I would rack up friendship points with these two when I moved back to the Valley Arms tomorrow.

Maxwell was right: the VIP seating in the garden boxes was so close to the stage, we were practically on it. The

Hollywood Bowl is an amphitheater in the Hollywood Hills that's kind of shaped like a bowl. The stage sort of looks like a giant seashell, and the audience seats are carved into the hillside facing it. Max told us about the history of the place. "All the greats have played here, from Ella Fitzgerald and Judy Garland to Diana Ross, Stevie Wonder, and Alicia Keys. There are seventeen thousand, five hundred seats, and tonight is completely sold out!"

Kashara leaned in close and whispered, "All those people just to see Destiny Manaconda? Even after she got fired from her show?"

I whispered back, "We don't know what really happened. And quit talking about it; Max is her manager." Kashara's eyes widened, and she zipped her lip, thank goodness.

There was a lot of press at the concert taking pictures of all the stars arriving. Kashara, Symphony, and I were trying hard not to gawk as stars like Lizzo, Common, Issa Rae, Dua Lipa, and Billie Eilish arrived. Mom didn't recognize most of them, but she was busy keeping an eye out for Tom Cruise and Idris Elba.

The show started with a film montage of Destiny's career. Then the Los Angeles Philharmonic Orchestra was revealed, and Destiny entered in a suit covered with so many sparkly crystals you almost had to shield your eyes when the lights hit her. The audience gave her a standing ovation before she'd even sung a note. Kashara, Symphony, and I held on to each other, keeping our squealing in check. TJ laughed and rolled his eyes, but midway into the show he was just as caught up in the excitement as the rest of us.

I was in awe how easily Destiny could perform, singing and keeping up with her dancers at the same time. It was obvious that she had to train and work extremely hard to make everything she was doing come off as effortless. I wondered if I could be that dedicated. Would it still seem like fun if I had to work so hard to be that good?

All concerts have a section when the artist gets intimate with the audience and sings a couple of ballads. Destiny's show followed that plan. They bought out a stool, lit her in a pool of light, and she sang her hit ballad, "Not Just Another Face in the Crowd." She was mesmerizing. The audience was over the moon cheering for her. She then asked for the house lights to be brought up. "Ladies and gentlemen, friends, thank you for all your support through the years. My next song was supposed to be a ballad that I fell in love with over the summer. It's from an Off-Off-Off-Broadway musical called *Yo, Romeo!*"

The mango pit in my stomach instantly transformed into a giant, state fair blue-ribbon size watermelon! Destiny continued, "It's a song sung by Romeo and Juliet called 'Duet Forever.' I could take a stab at it, but honestly, nobody sings it better than the two young performers who sang it in the play. And . . . they just so happen to be here tonight!"

Mom leaned on Dada as if she was going to faint. TJ clutched my hand so hard circulation ceased. Destiny put her hand over her eyes and scoped out the crowd until she found us. "There they are! My talented friends Mango Delight Fuller and TJ Gatt! Let's give them a hand and bring them up here to sing! Come on, you two!"

I was trembling. Max looked me in the eye and said, "This is it, Mango. The real test is happening right now." I took TJ's hand, and together we walked up the aisle and onto the stage. All the while I was thinking, *Is this what Max had been planning all along? Voza and the clothes and makeup and luxury he was showering us with were leading to this moment? I couldn't let him down. I couldn't let myself down.*

When we arrived onstage, Destiny handed both of us microphones and whispered, "Sky's the limit. Go for it!" Looking out at an audience of over seventeen thousand people, stars twinkling in the sky above us, cameras pointing at us, superstars watching us, and my heart thumping in my chest.

It was kind of surreal hearing my favorite song from *Yo, Romeo!* played by a full orchestra. I thought about Bob and Larry and how they would feel knowing their song was about to be heard at the Hollywood Bowl. I wanted to make them proud. TJ squeezed my hand, locked his kiwi-green eyes in with mine, and whispered, "It's just you and me. Nobody else is around." As the words left his lips, my voice came to mine, and I sang. I sang with all my heart because this was a moment I'd remember forever.

The entire audience rose to their feet at the end of the song. I don't know if they did this because we were that good or because we looked like two little kids on that huge stage, and they were giving us the *"aw shucks, ain't they cute"* appreciation ovation. Either way, it was beyond exhilarating. When we made it back to our seats, Mom was in tears. Dada's eyes were glistening, too. Max, smiling bright, gave us a thumbs-up. Kashara and Symphony were speechless as we approached, clutching each other's hands and making room for us as though we were Aladdin and Princess Jasmine landing on our magic carpet. I couldn't stop trembling; Dada was about to take off his jacket and put it around my shoulders, but TJ beat him to it. He put his arms around me to help stop my trembling, and I've honestly never felt closer to anyone outside my family in my life.

Backstage after the show, Destiny welcomed us to her dressing room. Photographers took pictures of Destiny, TJ, and me, as if we were stars, too. Soon famous people in the audience began to fill the dressing room. Max found me gawking in a corner and said, "Let's go, Mango. Your parents are already in the car. I want you to get some rest tonight. Tomorrow you've got an important meeting at Chrysalis Studio, and I want you at your best."

I felt like a zombie as he led me to the car. I'd just made my debut at the Hollywood Bowl, and first thing tomorrow I'd be meeting showbiz bigwigs. Had Max made all of this happen on purpose? Was this a part of his master plan? If so, I wished he would've let me in on it, then maybe the watermelon in my stomach wouldn't have turned into a ten-ton boulder!

CHAPTER FOURTEEN

Climb Every Hill

I was sleeping so deeply under the covers of the most comfortable cloud of a bed you could imagine. So, why did Jericka wake me at seven in the morning and practically drag me into the living room? I was so grumpy as I plopped down on the couch next to an equally grumpy Mom. Even Dada, the only "happy-in-the-morning person" in our family, had frown lines across his forehead. Then Jericka unmuted the television. There was an entertainment reporter on one of the morning shows reviewing Destiny's concert.

"Let me tell ya, folks, it was an unforgettable night. A true event. Destiny Manaconda nailed her place in Hollywood Bowl history." A clip of Destiny singing and dancing appeared on the screen, then back to the reporter. "And there was another surprise, folks. Destiny introduced the world to a couple of kids who won the hearts of everybody who was anybody in Hollywood last night!" A clip of TJ and me singing appeared on the screen. I screamed! Mom screamed! Dada jumped up, leaping from couch to couch screaming! I thought I was going to have a heart attack. TJ and I were on national television!

As Jericka gave us a "guided tour" of all the morning television shows, I couldn't believe TJ and I were mentioned again and again. A photograph we took with Destiny was featured on the cover of the *Los Angeles Times* style section and in the *Hollywood Reporter*. Mom got on the phone, calling Aunt Zendaya and all her friends back east. Dada was on Face2Face with relatives in Jamaica. When I finally picked up my phone, I had texts and messages from Izzy, Hailey Joanne, Bob, Larry, and just about everyone I knew from home. There was so much going on all around me, I was starting to hyperventilate.

Jericka took my hand, led me back to the bedroom, and sat down next to me on the bed. "It all seems to be happening too fast, doesn't it?"

I nodded. "Yeah, I guess. I mean . . . I don't know what's going on or how I feel."

"That's okay, Mango. Perfectly normal. While all the attention and applause are happening, I want you to think of it all as a tornado."

"A tornado?"

"That's right. You know how a tornado blows terrifically strong swirling winds that can uproot trees and blow away houses, but in the center of the tornado, right there in the middle of the storm, it's calm and peaceful. That's where you should aim to be. Right in the middle of the storm, not getting blown away or bothered by anything—negative or positive. You just keep your focus on what's in front of you, not what's happening around you, and you'll be all right."

Jericka ran a hot bath for me, scented with calming oils. She had a breakfast tray sent to my room and gave me the space to center myself. When it was time to prepare for the meeting at Chrysalis Studio, she brought in my outfit. I was expecting it to be something grown-up and professional, young, and cool, but she came in with the same clothes I wore on my first day in L.A. My shorts and T-shirt were washed and fresh, but I was surprised. "How come I have to wear this? Don't you think Voza should pick out something special for me?"

"This is what Max and Dionne want you to wear. Trust them; they know what they're doing."

Max hadn't let me down with his master plan so far. So, I got dressed, brushed my hair, pulled it back in my usual Afro puff, and joined Mom, Dada, and Jasper in Tabby's van and headed for the studio.

Max and Dionne were waiting outside an office tower on the studio lot. Dionne had a bright smile that made it clear to me that her dream of having her own show was definitely not over. Max had arranged for Mom, Dada, and Jasper to go on a behind-the-scenes tour of Chrysalis. "We'll all meet in my office later," Max said. "Enjoy the tour and lunch at the commissary."

I hugged my parents and planted so many smooches on Jasper's face that he laughingly pushed me away. Heading into the building with its marble floors, high ceilings, and banks of elevators, I said, "This place doesn't look anything like the rest of the lot."

"That's because this is where all the business part of *show business* takes place." Max took my hand. "All of the decisions involving money are handled upstairs on the top floors. When it comes down to it, it's not about who is the most talented, but who is the most marketable and profitable."

We stepped onto an elevator and Dionne said, "Don't worry about all that, Mango. Just relax and be yourself."

"Can I ask a question?"

Max smiled. "You just did, and yes, you can ask another one."

I gritted my teeth and then blurted, "Did Destiny get fired or quit the show?"

Max laughed as the door to the elevator opened. "That's ridiculous. Who told you that?"

"Well, Kashara and Symphony said that's what they heard."

Dionne sighed. "They ought to call this town Rumorwood instead of Hollywood."

Max agreed. "Don't believe the hype, kid. I'll fill you in on what's going on later, but right now, as far as you're concerned, this is it."

"That's what you said last night before I went on stage."

"Yes, and I meant it, too, for last night. Now there's a new hill in front of you. Can you climb it and get to the top like you did last night? If you do or *when* you do, there'll be another hill in front of you, and another after that, and that's how you build a career. Conquering one hill at a time, until you move on to the mountains. You ready?"

We stopped in front of a tall, dark mahogany door with the words "Conference Room A" in white letters. I thought about Jericka and what she said about being the calm in the center of the tornado. I closed my eyes for a second, took a calming breath, and said, "Yes, I'm ready."

CHAPTER FIFTEEN
Eyebrows

Walking into the conference room was like stepping into a movie. There was a long dark table surrounded by black leather chairs that swiveled and almost swallowed me up when I sat down. Seated around the table were ancient men with pink cheeks, white hair, and cold eyes. They didn't even crack a smile or show any reaction when Max introduced me. I gave a bright smile and waved at them; still no reaction.

The man at the head of the table had a shiny bald head, extremely thick, bushy, gray eyebrows, and no other hair on his face. Everyone in the room referred to him by his initials, "E.B." I wondered what the *E* and the *B* stood for. *Eye Brows?*

E.B. tapped his watch and said, "Let's get on with it."

Dionne stood and cleared her throat. "E.B., I'd like to start off showing you some film of Mango."

Now I wished the giant chair *would* swallow me. My screen test was awful! Why would Dionne show it to anyone unless she was trying to get me kicked out of Hollywood forever? But as the lights went down and a massive flat-screen TV rose from the end of the table, I was shocked. Dionne narrated as she showed footage she'd shot the day we met her—TJ and me playing around on the set. She kept talking about me being a regular girl with lots of energy and a fun personality that kids all over the world would identify with. "Mango has two very marketable qualities: her basic every girl personality AND her extraordinary vocal talent." The clip ended with me riding the bike into the pool and TJ and me having a splash war. There was a hum of comments around the room.

Maxwell showed a PowerPoint with a series of clips from the morning shows giving props to my performance at the Hollywood Bowl. (How did he put this all together so fast?) There were enlarged photos of TJ and me from the *L.A. Times* and the *Hollywood Reporter* and a bunch more from blogs I hadn't seen yet. And finally, reviews about my performance in the Off-Off-Off-Broadway production of *Yo Romeo!*

The lights came up and Max spoke. "E.B., you know me. We've made a fortune together. That's because I have a nose for talent. A nose, I might add, that has never failed me yet. This young lady is going to break big, so the question is, does her future lie with us here at Chrysalis or some other studio?"

The men around the table looked at each other, leaned in, and whispered comments. Eventually, E.B. looked across the conference table straight at me for the longest time, the furry caterpillars above his eyes moving in, up, down, and arching with his thoughts. I was so mesmerized with his brows, I smiled and said, "What up, Eyebrows?"

There was a moment of silence, then a smile spread across his face, and everyone in the room laughed. Eyebrows held his hand up, and the room went silent. "I saw you perform last night, young lady. I was very impressed. Not only by how you and young TJ sang together, but by the way the audience seemed to embrace you." He turned to Dionne, "Tell me, Ms. Harmony, how can a show designed for a big personality like Destiny fit this little girl? Unfortunately, I just don't see it."

Wait! What? Were they considering me for the lead in the show? I couldn't help it; my eyes popped out as I looked at Dionne. She came to stand next to me and put a reassuring hand on my shoulder. "That's just the thing, E.B., I'm revamping the show. Actually bringing it closer to the idea I pitched before Destiny was attached to the project. I wanted it to be about an ordinary girl in extraordinary circumstances. A girl any kid watching the show could identify with and then enjoy the fantasy of, as if it could happen to them, too."

E.B. spoke: "New scripts? A compete revamp? Is that what you're saying?"

"New scripts, new songs, Mango at the center with her best friend, TJ, by her side."

I couldn't help it, I gulped, and it was so loud, some of the men around the table turned to look at me. Embarrassing.

E.B., his face blank again, looked to Max, who said, "Imagine the impact it would have. The little girl who won the heart of Hollywood last night, signed to star in a Chrysalis TV show. The wave of publicity and goodwill would be worth millions. Come on now, E.B., jump on it. Let's ride the wave before it crests and we lose the momentum."

E.B. nodded, stood, and left the room with every other man around the table exiting right behind him, like a father goose and all his little goslings.

I turned to Max, "What do we do now?"

"Go back to my office and wait."

Max didn't just have an office, he had a bungalow, a series of offices for his management and production company. His private office was unexpected. The furnishing were modern, understated, and tasteful. The walls were mostly gray with white trim. All around, where you'd expect pictures of stars or posters from shows he worked on, there were paintings instead. Paintings by some of the African American artists I had learned about in school: Jacob Lawrence, Jean-Michel Basquiat, Kehinde Wiley, and more. I walked from painting to painting gawking, "Are these real?"

"If you're asking if they're originals, yes. The real deal."

"Wow, I didn't know you were an art lover."

"Well, I do enjoy art, but frankly, these paintings are an investment. The more established the artist, the older and rarer the painting, the more money they're worth. That Jacob Lawrence, for example, I could sell it today for ten to fifteen times what I paid for it ten years ago. My Basquiat is now worth more than my mansion, and my Kehinde Wiley will eventually be worth even more."

"Whoa, you should lock 'em in a vault somewhere."

"And not enjoy them? What would be the point of that?"

I thought it over and decided he was right. If you pay a lot of money for something, why not enjoy it while the value goes up? I decided that I would try to learn more about art and investing in it. I'd look around for something I really liked and hang it in my room. Of course, I'd have to take down some of my Beyoncé and Queen posters, but it'd be worth it.

I took a seat in front of Max's desk and twisted back and forth in the swivel chair. Max asked, "Something on your mind?"

"There's a million, gazillion things on my mind! But I guess the first thing is, if Dionne is changing the show to fit me, what about Destiny? Was she fired? Is she upset about it?"

Max laughed. "Remember I told you about building a career by climbing all the hills in front of you?"

"Yes."

"Well, Destiny has climbed to the top of each and every hill and now she's ready to tackle the mountains."

"Like French movie mountains?"

"Exactly, Davesh Muhammad Poitrine has cast her as the lead in his next film. It's an epic dramatic adventure that is going to be shot all over Europe for the next year and a half. Destiny couldn't pass up an offer like that. I wouldn't let her. It's been in the works for more than a year already. That's why we brought you out to L.A. You've been my backup plan since I saw you perform in New York. The studio agreed to release Destiny, but only if I found a viable replacement. You, my little Mango Delight, are the key to Destiny becoming a movie star."

"If Mr. E.B. says yes?"

"Exactly."

"What if he says no?"

"Then you go back home to your regular life, and I launch Plan C or D or E, or whatever plan I need to make things happen the way I want them to happen. I never give up. If I were the type to give up, I wouldn't have these paintings on my wall, would I?"

I nodded, unable to speak, because I was trying to understand how all these things were happening around me, for me, because of me, and to me AND could just as easily exclude me, and I had no idea. Maybe that was for the best, because if I had known what Max's plans were from the day we met, I might have been too scared to say yes to any of them. But could I really trust someone who was planning and thinking so far ahead? What if the things he planned for me didn't turn out to be things I wanted?

As we waited for my family to meet us at the office, I decided to keep a close eye on Max. If show business was a game, and Max knew how to play five steps ahead, I'd better be a sponge and learn how he did it. I didn't want to be a pawn or a puppet for Max or anyone else. If Mango Delight Fuller was in the game, she was gonna be a player.

CHAPTER SIXTEEN
A Seat at the Table

We were moved back to the Valley Arms (in a larger suite. since Mom and Jasper had arrived), and we waited for a decision from E.B. Max called to invite Mom and Dada to a lunch meeting with lawyers to talk "business." I said, "I want to go, too."

Max said, "This might be really boring for you, Mango. Why don't you hang out with your friends at the pool and let your parents handle things?"

"No, I'd rather hear stuff for myself, even if it is boring." Dada and Mom agreed that I could come along, and so I did. We met at the studio commissary in a private dining room. There was a lot food and discussion about money and con- tracts and record deals, and a lot of other details I couldn't wrap my head around, but . . . and this was a big BUT, none of it would happen if E.B. said no.

I was weary as Tabby drove us back to the Valley Arms. All the talk about percentages and contingencies and lawyerly lingo was boggling my mind. Mom and Dada were discussing the meeting, and I sort of tuned out until Dada said, "I don't get it. How can this E.B. guy have all the power?"

"What do you mean?" Mom said. "He ain't the only one with power. Ultimately, Mango has the power."

I perked up. "I do?"

"Yes, of course you do. These people are talking about contracts that would take years for you to fulfill. Your growing-up years, Mango. Just because this E.B., or whoever, says yes, it doesn't mean you can't say no."

"You'd let me decide?"

Dada said, "We'd talk about it as a family first, of course."

"Then get our own lawyer to look things over and guide us," Mom added.

"Right. Then we'd weigh the pros and cons and your mom and I would tell you what we think is best, but ultimately, . . . it's up to you, Mango-gal. Do you want this life or nah?"

I sat back in my seat and looked out the window. A part of me felt good about having to make the final decision. But then another part of me felt scared. I was just twelve, about to turn thirteen. What did I know about lawyers and contracts and committing to years of work? How could I be responsible for making a decision that could change my family's life forever? I liked my life the way it was back home, but I also liked what life could be in Hollywood. But did I like it enough? My eyelids were getting heavy. There was a lot of traffic, which made it a long ride back to the valley. I closed my eyes and drifted off to sleep.

Dionne took me out to lunch the next day. She wanted to pick my brain and get to know me better. We went to the Farmers Market next to the Grove in the Fairfax district. There were a whole bunch of different food stands to choose from. Dionne told me to go ahead and choose whatever I wanted, as much as I wanted. I was kind of hungry, so I got a slice of pineapple and pepperoni pizza, a falafel, a tamale, a chicken-and-steak skewer, saltwater taffy, a hunk of fudge, and I put dibs on an ice cream sundae for dessert.

I could see Dionne taking notes in her head as she watched me eat. She asked me a lot of questions as I took random bites of the food I chose. "What's your favorite color? What kind of movies do you like? Do you like to read? What kind of books? Who are your best friends? What do you look for when making friends?" The last question made me stop and think for a minute. I knew what I felt made friends, but I didn't really know how to put it into words yet. I needed more time to come up with an answer to that question. Maybe I would figure it out by checking in with my friends. I decided I was going to dedicate tonight to catching up with my girls. I didn't want to lose my besties in the middle of all the stuff going on.

When we were about to leave the Farmers Market, Dionne asked, "Is there anything you've been thinking about that you want to ask me?"

I did have a question that I'd been thinking about since we left the conference room the day before. "Dionne, how come there were no women or people who looked like you, me, or Max in that room with Eyebrows?"

"Good question, Mango." Dionne sat back and looked at me closely. "Right now in Hollywood those guys are the ones who make most of the decisions. There are a few women in positions of power here and there, but not enough. People like Max and me and you have made it into the room with these guys. We have the product. They're beginning to understand that our stories are important and make money all around the world. They have to include us now if they want to remain successful. Every time we succeed, we're closer to getting a seat at that table. We're making a way for more women and people of color to be the decision makers in those conference rooms. We're on a mission to change things, Mango, and you're a part of that. We're playing the long game. You down?"

I said, "Yeah!" and we bumped fists across the table. Then I thought of another question, "If E.B. says yes, what happens then?"

"We go straight to work. While I'm jamming on the new scripts, you go into preparation and training mode. We're going to put together a team to prepare you."

"What's that mean?"

"Well, we'll hire an acting coach to help you with scripts and acting technique. We'd bring in a vocal coach to keep your voice in shape and get you used to recording in a studio.

The studio would bring in a publicist for media training . . ."

"What's that?"

"That's where we teach you how to do interviews and talk to the press about the show. Then we'd put your glam squad together for wardrobe fittings, hair and makeup tests and photo sessions, and more."

"Will TJ have to do all this stuff, too?"

"Well, maybe not as much as you, the star of the show carries the heaviest load, but both of you will be extremely busy during what we call pre-production. Then in about six weeks we'd begin shooting the show. I don't mean to scare you off, Mango, but it's a lot."

I decided to pass on the ice cream sundae. With so much to think about, I didn't want to risk a stomachache. I thought about Destiny and how all the people closest to her were on her "team." Would it be the same for me? Would my team become my closest friends?

Then Dionne's phone and my phone rang at the same time. It was Max's office for Dionne, and Mom calling me. Eyebrows had made a decision.

CHAPTER SEVENTEEN

Cheesy Charms

Izzy's face appeared on my phone almost before the first buzz finished, "Mango! I've been waiting for your call. I knew it was gonna come today. You know, sometimes I think I'm part psychic like my late great-aunt Maria Magdalena, who predicted her own death. Something told me, *don't move five inches from your phone all day, because Mango is gonna call with news.* That's why I could answer on the first ring, because I just KNEW you would call today! What happened? Did you find out yet?"

"Hold on, Izzy, I'm gonna connect Hailey Joanne." My hands were shaking, I was so nervous and excited. It was hard for me to touch the icon that would add Hailey Joanne to the Face2Face with Izzy.

Her phone rang and rang, and just before I thought it'd say she was unavailable, she appeared on screen. "Mango, hey, guess what? Hervé sent me a gift all the way from Paris!"

"He did? What is it?"

"A charm for my charm bracelet."

"Get out!"

"It's so sweet. It's gold and in the shape of a wedge of cheese!"

"Cheese? Seriously?"

"Yes, it's so sweet. He knows how much I adore cheese!"

Izzy broke in. "Hello? Who cares about ya little cheesy charm? Mango's got news!"

"Well, excuse me, Isabel," Hailey Joanne snapped. "Some of us have lives, too, you know."

"Your life with the cheese guy I can live without. Mango's living a true Hollywood story, and I want the tea!"

"Maybe I should just hang up, and you can call me later, Mango."

"Yeah, maybe you should!"

"No, no, no! Wait! I want to tell my best friends together, at the same time. Please!"

Izzy shrugged. "Okay. I'll chill if she'll chill."

Hailey Joanne rolled her eyes. "Consider moi froid, that's chill en français."

Now that the peace treaty between my two warring besties had been signed, I took a deep breath and said, "We have a green light. They picked up the show!"

There was a burst of screaming. Both Hailey Joanne and Izzy dropped their phones and leapt around their rooms. I was leaping around my room, too. I was excited in Max's office when he told my family and me the answer was yes, but it was different now. I was sharing it with my friends, the ones who really counted, and so it was like hearing it the first time all over again—but better.

Izzy was in tears when she picked up her phone again. "Oh. Mango, I'm so happy for you, chica! Nobody in the world could ever be happier for you than me!"

Hailey Joanne broke in. "Pardonnez-moi, Isabel, it's just like you to gobble up all the happiness in the world."

"Gobble up? Are you making a crack about my weight, Hateful Jo?"

"How dare you call me that!"

"How dare you body-shame me!"

"STTTOOOPPP! If you two don't try to get along I'm gonna hang up."

"Sorry, Mango."

"Yeah, me too. I'm sorry," Izzy said. "I'm just so happy for you. And I'm so glad you chose to tell me first."

"Me too," Hailey Joanne said. "When are you coming home? I'm gonna throw the biggest party for you!"

"Hailey Joanne, that's a great idea! Can I help plan it? I can get the gang from school, and we can see if they'll let us hold it in the auditorium at school!"

"Auditorium, no way! I'll get Mom to rent the ballroom at the Rivoli."

"OMGZ, that would be mega-uber-awesome!"

I was so touched that my two besties were excited for me and fired up about throwing a party for me, but I had to dump a bucket of cold water on their plans. "Hey, you two, I can't come home for a party. There's no time."

"What do you mean?"

"Eyebrows only gave us four weeks instead of six to begin shooting the show, so it's ready to premiere on the same schedule as it was when Destiny was in it. I don't even have a minute to breathe."

"But what about school? What about your parents? What about your clothes?"

"TJ and I are going to have a tutor. Dada's flying back tomorrow to gather our things and close up the apartment for six months, and . . ." I couldn't help it, all the feelings about my home, my friends, my real life, and all the things I'd be missing began pushing up into my eyes, and a flood of tears poured out.

Hailey Joanne and Izzy did their best to reassure me that we wouldn't lose touch and we'd be friends forever, but I couldn't stop sobbing. Then they were sobbing, too. We said goodnight, sniffing and blowing our noses. I fell asleep with salty tears rolling down my cheeks.

CHAPTER EIGHTEEN

Fossils

Mom and Dada hired Maria Perez-Blue as our lawyer. She was a high-energy Latina who came highly recommended by TJ's dad, Malachi. He was a corporate lawyer and he'd hired her to represent TJ. Ms. Perez-Blue drove a Jaguar and wore stylish tailored suits and stiletto heels. At first, Mom wasn't sure about TJ and me having the same lawyer, and she was concerned about the lawyer's feet. "Anyone who wears heels that high must spend a lot of time sitting on her butt."

Ms. Perez-Blue took Mom and me out for lunch at that Versailles restaurant Symphony and Kashara had raved about. They were right, the garlic chicken was a delicacy from poultry heaven. It turned out Ms. Perez-Blue was a Puerto Rican from New York. She and Mom had a similar no-nonsense energy and a rapid-fire way of talking and getting right to the point. She assured us, "Don't worry, I know the Hollywood game, and I play it better than everyone else.

My six-inch heels make sure I stand eye-to-eye with the boys' club, and I'm not to be ignored or taken lightly. Trust me, when I finish making your deal, you'll know I'm worth my fifteen percent."

After Maria (she insisted we call her by her first name) dropped us off at the Valley Arms, Mom said, "She's a tough negotiator like me. I ain't worried no more. She's gonna get the best deal out of Max and Chrysalis Studios."

I was disappointed when I found out Jericka was being reassigned to help prepare Destiny for a year and a half of location shooting in Europe. Jericka was replaced by Demonica Osborne. Max said, "Demonica has been with Maxwell Paige Entertainment since I started the company. I usually personally manage my newest clients, but since I'll be spending most of my time abroad with Destiny, Demonica will handle you just as well, if not better, than I would."

The thing about Demonica was, well, she was like Mom on steroids. She even looked like an older version of Mom. No makeup, no fussy clothing, and severely sensible shoes. Demonica immediately took my phone and downloaded the week's schedule into my calendar and set a six o'clock wake-up time for me every day except Sundays. "Why do I have to get up so early?"

"May as well get used to it now. Once you start shooting, you'll have to be in hair and makeup by six. For now, you'll swim laps in the pool daily. Then, after a high protein breakfast I personally designed to increase my clients' energy, we'll begin your appointments."

"Appointments?"

"Acting, singing, media training, fittings, grooming, etiquette, and tutoring. We won't have a moment to waste."

My alarm barked at six on the dot. The ringtone Demonica chose was harsh and unrelenting. I took a quick shower and got into the swimsuit that Demonica had laid out the night before. She buzzed my phone. "I'm at the pool waiting. Let's go!" I hustled into my robe, down the stairs (the elevator in the Valley Arms was notoriously slow), and out into the frigid morning air. "I'm freezing!"

"You won't be by the fifteenth lap. The quicker you dive in, the faster you'll get over the icy shock."

She practically pushed me into the water, and as I swam back and forth, lap after lap, she timed me with an app on her phone. Climbing out of the water, I saw she was shaking her head at me. "Not bad, but you can do a lot better." I trembled and frowned. Demonica noticed and said, "You'll thank me once you've built up the stamina to sing and dance for hours without breaking a sweat. I took charge of Destiny when she started touring, and look at her now."

Maybe she had a point. I mean, Destiny was a beast onstage. She made everything look easy, even when she was working her butt off. After my reshower, Demonica had my breakfast waiting for me, a pre-portioned high-pro tray that she put in the microwave for exactly forty-six seconds. The plant-based bacon, powdered eggs, and dried fish jerky may have been high in protein, but they were beyond low in taste. Thank goodness she handed me a fruit-and-vitamin smoothie that actually tasted good.

Demonica's SUV was a shrine to her love of cats. There were cat air fresheners; four cat bobbleheads on the dashboard; a cat compass with whiskers that pointed north, south, east and west; cat stuffed animals across the back seat; and a giant cat plush toy in the front passenger seat strapped in with the seat belt. I guessed I was supposed to ride in the back, and I was right, "The back seat gives you more room to stretch out, go over your lines, or answer fan mail when it comes to that."

We arrived at the Falmouth Laboratory Actors' Technique Studio or FLATS at ten o'clock. I was scheduled to have sessions with Rory Falmouth three times a week for three hours each day. We would cover improvisation, acting technique, camera technique, and script analysis. Rory Falmouth took himself very seriously. He had a paunch that proceeded him as he moved, because he kept his weight on his heels. He wore a blond toupee that swooped down low over his forehead. His voice was high-pitched and nasal, almost whiny, but Demonica swore he was the best in the business, so I went along with it.

Rory took me on a tour of the dingy studio, pointing out framed black-and-white photographs of himself playing various roles in outdoor theater productions of Shakespeare when he was about four decades younger. He said his camera acting technique was perfected when, "I starred as Doctor

Herman Humanitas in the classic soap opera *The Days of Our Months*. We only lasted two seasons, but our show took the soap opera artform to new levels—everyone says so."

I was the only student for the first two hours, and then a group of longtime students of Rory's joined us for improvisation. They treated him like he was the inventor of the Academy Awards and gold statuettes fell from his mouth every time he spoke. Rory was nice until it was time to critique work, then he'd sharpen his tongue and carve you up like a Thanksgiving turkey. "I don't believe you! You're faking! Acting is reacting! You've got the emotional range of sawdust! Are you a human or a robot? I can't tell."

When it came to camera technique, Rory would play a scene where I was on camera and he would read the scene partner lines off camera. At the end of the scene he would always make me take a long pause before he called "cut" and then would instruct me on how to pause. "As the camera moves in for a close-up, you must think real thoughts that speak through your face. 'Did I leave my iron on this morning? I can't remember if I shut it off or not. Oh dear, I hope I don't set my home on fire!'" These thoughts would register, and the camera would record true emotion.

As if that wasn't bad enough, Rory Falmouth was a real foul-mouth. He'd come up close to whisper directions in my ear, and his breath smelled like sour cream and onion potato chips. Old sour cream and onion potato chips. They used to be my favorite chips, and now I never wanted to eat them again.

After our second session the first week, I couldn't take it anymore. I asked Demonica if there was another teacher I could study with, and she said, "Don't be ungrateful. Rory Falmouth is one of the most respected acting coaches in the industry. I studied with him when I first started out, and so did Selma La Toure, may she rest in peace. Rory was the first serious acting coach to integrate his studio! Black, White, Asian, and Latin actors, we formed our own company all because of Rory Falmouth. So, please, young-lady-with-a-lot-to-learn, show some respect for Rory, your craft, and yourself!"

She made me feel microbe small. Maybe I was judging Rory too quickly. I decided to give him another try. Maybe rubbing some of Mom's wintergreen essential oil under my nose would kill the sour cream and onion funk.

My vocal couch, Naomi Metropolis, was another one of Demonica's dear friends. They shared a love of cats. Naomi had four, two of which sat on the upright piano, meowing along as we practiced scales. The third one sat in Naomi's lap, looking very judgmental. The fourth, an overstuffed calico, wove in and out between my ankles as I tried to stand with my knees bent and my back straight—so my breath would drop directly into my diaphragm. I don't think I got to sing a song at all in the ninety-minute sessions. Naomi was so insistent on my learning to sing in my head voice, all I did was exercises that had me sounding like an owl auditioning for the Metropolitan Opera. I "hooted" up and down the scales, trying to imagine my voice coming through a hole in my forehead just above my nose.

Dada was back at home, sending clothes and things to L.A. by mail and closing up our apartment, so I complained to Mom, but she wasn't having it. "Look, Mango, this is what you chose when you said yes. Once you make a choice you have to stick with it, like I've always taught you."

On the third night, I made a Face2Face call with Hailey Joanne and Izzy again. This time they didn't get a chance to fight each other, because I was too busy spilling my guts about Demonica, Rory, Naomi, and the overfed calico cat. Izzy was sympathetic, "Oh, Mango, you poor thing! I wish I could give you a hug."

"She doesn't need a hug," Hailey Joanne broke in. "What she needs is some guts. If you don't like these has-beens, speak up! Tell Max or whomever you want to get rid of them and demand better!"

Izzy said, "You're gonna make her sound like a diva!"

"Divas are stars! Divas are bosses! What's wrong with that? You know Mango's always had a problem speaking up for herself."

"I know, but that's her personality; she is who she is."

"No, I'm not who I is! I mean, I'm not who I *was!*" I shouted, "I've changed! I've learned a lot dealing with you two!"

"Well, act like it then!" Hailey Joanne snapped back at me. "Don't come to us whining and complaining. Go to someone who can do something about it and tell them what you want. That's the only way you'll get it. The squeaky wheel gets the grease, girl!"

Izzy said, "Squeaky wheels can also get replaced."

"True, but that's a chance you'll have to take, Mango."

I had called my friends for compassion, and what I got was the ice-cold truth about myself. I was falling back into old habits. Going along to get along. Trying not to make waves and avoid conflict. When was I ever going to learn to stand up for myself? Just because Demonica and her friends were professionals didn't mean they knew what was right for me. But did I know? I spent the rest of the night until I fell asleep reaching deep inside myself searching for answers to what I really wanted and needed.

I woke up at five-thirty, beating my blaring alarm, and called Max. He answered the phone not sounding sleepy at all, "Max here. What is it, Mango?"

"Max, we need to, I mean, I want to have a meeting. With you."

"Let me check my schedule."

"It's an emergency, Max."

"Okay. Give me an hour; I'll be there."

Once I hung up with Max, I made the same call to Maria Perez-Blue, Dionne Harmony, and Jericka. I woke Mom and told her to get ready for a meeting. "What? Who? Why is anybody having a meeting this early? What in the world is going on?"

"I'm standing up for myself, Mom, like you always told me to. So, get ready." Then I jumped into a hot shower, practicing what an wanted to say as if it were lines in a script. I was determined to make things right for me!

CHAPTER NINETEEN

Girl Boss

I put on a pot of coffee for my "guests." I don't drink coffee yet, although I wish I did, but Mom said it would stunt my growth. My legs were almost twice as long as my torso, and maybe my growth needed to be stunted, but Mom wouldn't hear of it. Still, I knew how to make a good pot of coffee even if I couldn't drink it. I loved the smell, so on the rare days that I got up early on my own, I'd have a pot of coffee brewing for Mom and Dada.

I wanted to be taken seriously, so I put on the only dress I had in L.A. (Dada promised boxes of our clothes would be arriving from home soon), and I ordered muffins and a fruit plate from room service. I set out cups, small plates, napkins, and utensils on the table in the kitchenette.

Max arrived first. "You want to tell me what this is all about?"

"Yes, I will, Max, as soon as everyone else gets here."

"Everyone else? Who? What? . . ."

"Would you like some coffee, Max? You take it black, don't you?"

He sputtered something about nonsense as I placed a cup of black coffee and a lemon-poppyseed muffin with icing on the coffee table in front of him. I'd been watching Max. I knew what he liked, and I'd also learned how to butter him up the way he did when he was easing his clients into his master plan. He took a sip and looked at the cup with raised eyebrows, as if he were surprised. "*Mmm*, good coffee."

Mom came in and greeted Max. He said, "Do you know what's going on here, Marjorie?"

"Your guess is as good as mine, Max." She got a cup of coffee, stared at the muffins, thought better of it, shook her head, and took a seat. "You'd better hurry up and get this started, Mango, before your brother wakes up and gets to running around this *little place* like a hurricane."

Hmmm. I could see Mom was dropping hints with her "little place" comment. Our three rooms at the Valley Arms were half the size of our apartment back home, but she didn't need to worry, I had her back.

Max separated the top from the bottom of his muffin. He only ate the muffin tops, his way of keeping himself disciplined. He said, "Where's Demonica? Shouldn't you be with her by now?"

"I . . . um . . . I gave her the day off." Actually, I had told her I was sick and very contagious, so she went home and said she'd check in with me later.

Maria, Dionne, and Jericka arrived one right after the other. Once they were settled with their coffee and muffins, I stood facing them all. I took a moment to slow my breathing. I reminded myself I'd come a long way from the girl throwing up in the bathroom at school and getting into all sorts of messes because I was afraid of confrontation. I was just about ready to start talking when Max checked his watch and said, "Well . . . ?"

Maria held her hand up. "Give her a chance to gather her thoughts, Maxwell." She looked at me. "Take your time, Mango. Tell us what's on your mind."

I saw Mom smile and throw an appreciative nod Maria's way. I relaxed. "I called you all here because I need to make some changes. I want to do my best as an actor, singer, and everything else I'm responsible for doing, but I'm not happy with my team."

Max threw his hands in the air. "Are you kidding me? Really? This diva business starting already?" He got up from the couch as if to leave.

Jericka held her hand out to him and said, "Dad, remember, 'It's our job to listen to our clients with respect.'"

"She's twelve years old!"

"Twelve-and-three-quarters," I said.

Dionne snickered. Max sighed and sat back down. Mom said, "Go on, honey."

"As I was saying, I want some changes so I can do my best." I looked at Maria, "And I want these changes in my contract." Maria nodded, reached into her bag, and took out a notepad.

I continued, "I don't think Demonica Osborne is a good fit for me. I need a different manager."

"Oh, so you're going to tell me my business now?" said Max. "Like you know better than I do?"

"No! I mean . . . everyone makes mistakes, and you just made one choosing Demonica to work with me when you have a much better choice already working for you."

"Who, young lady?"

"Jericka. She's the best. I want her to manage me while you're gone."

Mom chimed in, "Yes! We love Jericka!"

"It's not about who you love; it's about who you need. Jericka's not ready to manage talent full time."

"Yes, I am, Max."

"'Max?' Since when are you calling me by my first name?"

"Since I want you to take me seriously. I'm ready. I think I've proven myself again and again. I can do way more than pack Destiny's clothes and review her itinerary. It's time for you to see that, or I'll have to move on to another company that can see my worth."

Max leaned back in his seat as if Jericka had thrown a flaming bowling ball into his lap. "I built this business for you!"

"I know that, and I appreciate it, but I'm ready to be promoted so I can do what you've trained me to do."

Max thought for a minute then looked at me and said,

"All right, Jericka, I'll promote you to be Mango's manager—on a trial basis. We'll see how ready you are."

Jericka beamed. "Thank you, Max."

Max bristled and turned to me. "Is that it?"

"No, there's more. I don't want Rory Falmouth or Naomi Metropolis on my team anymore."

"Who?" Max said.

"The people Demonica hired to coach me in acting and singing. They . . . well . . . they're kind of outdated. Naomi makes me sing along with her cats, and Rory smells like sour cream and onion potato chips."

Max slapped his thighs. "Well, if this isn't the—"

Maria interrupted, "Repeat their names Mango. I want to exclude them in your contract." I repeated their names and their jobs slowly.

"Well, Mango Delight Fuller . . ." Max popped the last of his poppyseed muffin top into his mouth and chewed slowly while we waited. "Since you've dismantled your team, do you have any replacements besides Jericka?"

"Yes, I do." I handed Jericka a slip of paper with two names and phone numbers. "Bob Levy and Larry Ramsey are my teachers from school. Bob teaches drama, and Larry is a music teacher and vocal coach. They wrote *Yo, Romeo!* and discovered me. I feel like I'd get much further faster working with them, because we know each other and I trust them."

"This is outrageous. Schoolteachers?"

"But you liked them, Max. You said you liked the show.

You had me sing one of their songs at the Hollywood Bowl."
I turned to Dionne. "I was thinking they could write some of
the new songs for the series. Songs that fit me."

Dionne nodded. "I loved the song you and TJ sang at the
Bowl. I'll consider it."

Jericka said, "What if they're back teaching and not
available?"

"They told me they weren't going back to school this year.
They were going to be full-time artists. Will you call them
and see if they're available, please?"

"Of course, I'll reach out and circle back as soon as I hear
from them."

Max said, "Well, Mango, now that you've sprung your
little coup d'état, may I leave?"

"Just one more thing." I looked at Mom. "This place is
really too small for the four of us. Dada is sending our clothes
and things we need from home, including Jasper's highchair,
stroller, and toys. My little brother needs space to play, and
he can't nap during the day because of the constant noise
from the pool . . . so . . ."

"All right, I knew this was coming. Jericka, find your
client a more appropriate domicile."

"I believe I already have, Max."

"Really? Where?"

Jericka smiled. "Destiny's home will be vacant for more
than a year. The Fullers can lease it—at a friends and family
rate."

Maria chimed in, "You'll notice there's a request for a substantial relocation bonus in our response to your contract. The studio can't expect this family to move all the way across country on their own dime. The bonus we're requesting should cover a good chunk of the lease."

I couldn't believe it. I was going to live in Destiny Manaconda's amazing house. This was beyond! Those massive rooms. The views of the city. Blackout windows! A pool! Patios! Fruit trees! Mom was going to flip when she saw it. Jasper would have room to play, and I could teach him to swim, and the pool was heated, so I wouldn't have to freeze doing my laps in the morning!

Max stood up to leave. "Okay, whatever you want. I've got business to take care of. Jericka, anything else you report back to me. Just because you're a full manager now doesn't mean I'm not the boss."

Jericka said, "Yes, Max."

Max flinched as if his ear ached. "Aren't you ever going to call me Dad again?"

"Yes, Max, but not while we're working."

Max sighed and headed for the door. I followed him. "Max, are you going to let Demonica go today?"

"You mean fire her?"

"Yes."

"No. I'm not going to do that. Since you're twelve-and-three-quarters and powerful enough to make your demands and rebuild your team, you fire her."

"Huh? Me?"

"I'll call her from my car and tell her you want to see her right away. You fire her yourself and see what it feels like to really be in charge. You've got to pay the cost to be the boss, Mango."

He smiled that big grin of his, the one where I could see the wheels turning in his brain. His smile grew brighter as he stepped into the hall, his eyes never leaving mine until the door was shut.

I knew Max was kind of paying me back for making so many demands of him, but I didn't mind. I was ecstatic! I'd gotten everything I wanted, including a home in the West Hollywood Hills. Now the only thing I had to worry about was firing Demonica. Maybe I could get Jericka to do it, but no, that would be avoiding confrontation, and I wasn't going to do that anymore.

CHAPTER TWENTY

Beyond!

After the meeting, Mom was busy getting Jasper fed, bathed, and dressed for the day when Demonica called. "I hear you're feeling better. Ready for me to come back?" I asked her to meet me at noon by the pool. She said, "It'll be too crowded to do your laps freely, but okay, I'll figure out something to make it worthwhile." So she was still expecting us to continue with the schedule. I guess Max didn't fill her in on what was going on, which meant I'd really have to let her go on my own.

I didn't want to do it over the phone; that would be the coward's way out. I had to do this face to face. I remembered Mom talking about letting people go as a part of her management duties at Target. She always said, "I take them to a place where there are a lot of people. A restaurant or a mall. People are less likely to act a fool if there's a crowd around." That's why I decided noon at the pool would be the perfect place to fire Demonica.

I walked into the pool area exactly at twelve o'clock. Symphony and Kashara were in the pool and waved frantically with bright smiles on their faces. I nodded then headed directly toward Demonica, who was standing near the diving board with her stopwatch. A look of surprise came across her normally stone face when she saw I was wearing my dress. "What's with the outfit? We've got work to do."

"Demonica, we need to talk. Let's find a place to sit down—"

"I'd rather stand. I sit more than enough chauffeuring you all around town."

The mango pit in my stomach made its presence known, and I decided to just get this over with before it kept growing. "Demonica, it's not you, really. I mean, it's totally me, but this relationship is not working out, and I'm gonna have to let you go."

"Let me go? Go where?"

"Go back to what you used to do before Max put us together, I guess. Jericka Paige is going to manage me from now on. It's just a better fit."

"And Max knows about this?"

"Yes. We discussed it this morning."

Demonica grimaced, sucking in air between her clenched teeth. "All right. Fine. Yeah, I'm a tough cookie, but my methods create stars. Ask Destiny Manaconda. On second thought, don't ask Destiny or any of the stars I've built brick by brick. You only get one chance with Demonica Osborne, and you blew it. Good luck."

She turned to walk away as Kashara and Symphony climbed out of the pool, almost knocking Demonica into the water. Kashara grabbed her arm before she fell. "Oh my goodness! I'm sorry, lady. I'm just so excited."

"Really?" Demonica snarled as she barreled toward the parking lot. "Well, whoop-de-doo for you!"

Kashara said, "What's with her?"

I shrugged. "She's having a bad day, I guess. So, what are you so excited about?"

"We're both excited," Symphony said, turning to me. "I got a callback again at Chrysalis!"

"I did too," Kashara squealed. "I knew they didn't forget me!" She flipped her box braids. "This is not the look of a girl you forget, *okuuurrr*!"

"That's great. What's the callback for?"

Symphony said, "We're not sure. We thought it was for the Destiny Manaconda project, but we heard that's dead."

"Maybe they changed it . . ." Kashara gasped, lifting a hand to her mouth, ". . . and one of us could be replacing Destiny!"

"OMG, I've got a feeling you're right!" Symphony said, grabbing Kashara's hands and squealing, "I bet it's you. You would be so perfect as Destiny!"

"No! It's gonna be you, I just know it, girl! You're way more Destiny than I'll ever be."

I just watched as they turned and headed back to the pool, gassing each other up. I didn't know if I was supposed to say anything yet. No announcements had been made, and no contracts had been signed. I decided it was better to keep things to myself for now.

I changed into my usual jeans and T-shirt and was making a grilled cheese and tomato sandwich when Jericka arrived. "We've got to go shopping, Mango. Voza Clyde is already pulling outfits on Rodeo Drive."

Rodeo Drive was the most exclusive area to shop in Beverly Hills. Of course, I wanted to go there, but I'd been up since before sunrise and I was hungry and tired. "Why right now?"

"Because the studio is making the big announcement about your being cast to play the lead in the new series tomorrow. You're going to be interviewed on *Top of the Day L.A.* at seven-thirty in the morning, then there'll be a press junket and a series of satellite interviews from all around the country before we pre-record a spot on *Entertainment America* that'll run in the evening."

I got a feeling in my stomach, but I couldn't decide if it was hunger or nerves. I opted for hunger. "Uh . . . can I eat first?"

"Bring it with you to the car; we've got to go!"

I wrapped my sandwich in a paper towel, gave Mom and Jasper quick pecks on the cheek, and headed for the door. Mom called out, "Nothing too expensive or grown-up now! They've got nice things for tweens at Target, too!"

Ugh! Tweens! That was a word and a label I would be happy to be rid of in a few weeks. My birthday was coming up, and I'd finally be a teen. The "w" would be gone for good.

The "w" meant you were "in betWeen" being a little kid and a TEENAGER! Being a teen was a major step in life. One step closer to being able to drive. One step closer to being able to date. One step closer to being able to get a part-time job and get paid. One step closer to going to college. One step closer to being an adult (yeah, "being an adult" was still far away, but getting closer to it counted!).

I followed Jericka, my warm sandwich in my hand oozing cheese and juicy tomato onto the paper towel, to a long, shiny red convertible. I'd never seen a car like it before. "Cool car! What kind is it?"

"It's 1967 Chevrolet Impala. A classic. Max has seventeen classic cars."

"Seventeen!"

"Yep. All of them a different shade of red. He calls this one Ketchup."

"Where does he keep seventeen cars?"

"He has a garage under the house that's climate controlled to protect the exterior paint. He's sort of a car fanatic. If you ever want to get on his good side, compliment his taste in cars."

That was good to know. I added it to my list of facts about the things Max liked:

Good black coffee

Lemon-poppyseed muffin tops

African American fine art

Classic cars in shades of red

As we headed for Beverly Hills, I chomped down my sandwich, careful not to get any melted cheese or crumbs on the upholstery. I kept Jericka talking about all seventeen of Max's cars, trying to learn as much as I could for later use.

Shopping with Voza was a ton of fun. His camera crew followed us everywhere. Jericka explained that it was a part of my duties to promote the show. At first I felt weird with the cameras all around and the boom mic floating overhead, but Voza said, "Ignore them, Mango-tango. Think of them as mannequins in the store, and be your fabulous self."

After a while, I did forget they were there and went along with Voza's fabulization of everything he considered *beyond trend*. "We don't follow trends, Mango-tango, we set the trends and let the universe follow, because we are beyond!"

The prices in the stores on Rodeo Drive were *beyond ridiculous*. A twelve hundred dollar T-shirt! A three thousand dollar pair of jeans! Everything I owned was from the sale rack at Target. Mom was going to freak out! I was afraid to say I liked anything until Jericka whispered in my ear, "We're not buying the clothes; the designers are lending them to us for promotional purposes." That meant Mom wouldn't have to pay for the clothes, and I didn't get to keep them. I just had to remember who designed what, so when reporters asked, "Who are you wearing?" I would say the name of the designer. I calmed down and stopped imagining Mom as one of those giant balloons in the Thanksgiving Day Parade hovering over my head chanting, "They've got nice things for tweens at Target, too!"

The trunk of the sixty-seven Chevy was loaded with garment bags, a separate labeled bag for each outfit I was to wear during the next day's press tour.

7AM/*Top of the Morning*/Lumiere striped jumpsuit
   w/Charisse aubergine blouse/faux emerald stud
   earrings/cuff bracelet.

8AM-NOON/Curtiza black jeans/LaScaza silk T-shirt/
   Carouso studded leather harness/red velours
   pumps/Donatello earrings and bracelet set.

There were three more specifically labeled garment bags. Voza instructed, "Just put on exactly what I've set out in each bag and remember the designers. Easy-peasy, Mango-tango." I didn't know why Voza kept calling me Mango-tango, but I didn't mind it from him. He was high energy and so friendly. I started liking the sound of it.

On the drive back to the Valley Arms, Jericka pretended she was a reporter and asked me a lot of questions. "Are you excited to be the star of a new show?"

"Yes."

"What do you think of L.A.?"

"It's nice."

"Do you think your life will change now?"

"Probably."

Jericka pulled into the Valley Arms parking lot. I was ready to jump out of the car to show Mom the price tags on the clothes and pretend we had to pay for them. It was too good a practical joke to pass up. But Jericka asked me to wait a while; we needed to talk.

"All the questions I was asking you, Mango, are the kinds of questions you'll be asked all the time starting tomorrow."

"Okay. Cool."

"Well, one- or two-word answers are not exactly cool."

"Why?"

"It's your job to be interesting. So the people watching get to share your experiences. Live the fantasy they imagine you're living."

"How do I do that?"

"I'll text you a list of questions tonight. I want you to think about making your answers interesting by adding a touch of the personal. For example, if you're asked what you think of Los Angeles, how could you answer in a more colorful and specific way?"

I bit my bottom lip. It took me a moment, trying to come up with a good answer. I said, "I love the weather, and there's lots of stuff to do, like the amusement parks and the beaches and stuff."

"That's good. You might also want to mention your favorite ride at an amusement park, or what it was like to see the Pacific Ocean for the first time, or something fun that happened at the beach. Tonight I want you to think about each question I send and how you'd answer it with more than one or two words. We'll go over them in the morning, so get a good night's rest."

"Is TJ going to be at the interview, too?"

"Oh no. TJ's flying back home for a few days."

"What?" He never mentioned that to me. Then again, when would he? He was busy spending time with his dad, and I was busy with everything going on in my life. We'd barely had any time to even talk on the phone since we'd arrived in L.A. Now, to find out he was on his way home. Why did he get to go home and not me? "That's not fair. He gets to go home and I don't?"

"His mother wants him there for her wedding."

"Oh yeah, I forgot about that."

"Another thing you need to think about, Mango. You're playing the lead in the show. Your workload is going to be a lot heavier than TJ's or any of your other cast mates. Understand?"

I nodded and squeaked out, "Yes."

"Okay. Let's take these garment bags up to your room. You get a good night's rest, and I'll pick you up at five in the morning, dressed and ready to roll."

Five? That was earlier than Demonica! I had a feeling Jericka was going to be way tougher as a manager than she was as an assistant. She had a lot to prove to Max, and I was the guinea pig she was going to prove it with. What had I done? Created a manager monster? A monsta-ger?

CHAPTER TWENTY-ONE

Cinderella Story?

I was up and ready to roll when Jericka arrived at exactly five in the morning, but I felt like a zombie. I kept bumping into things as I made my way around the apartment. Mom got up early to make sure I was ready. The cool thing was, she gave me a couple of sips of her coffee to give me a much needed boost. Yum!

Today, Jericka was *rolling* in a vintage Corvette Stingray. It was dark out, so I couldn't tell what shade of red the car was, but Jericka said, "Max calls this one Pomegranate," so I had a pretty good idea what it'd look like when the sun came up.

My morning face was super puffy from sleep, so as soon as I was seated, Jericka handed me a cold compress mask that completely covered my face except for mouth and eye holes. "It'll make the puffiness go away by the time we get you into hair and makeup.

"By the way, I've hired a glam squad for this morning. If you feel comfortable with them, we'll keep them on as a part of Team Mango." I liked the way *Team Mango* sounded, and I especially liked the fact that Jericka was including me in decisions about whom I'd be working with. Not that anyone could tell, but I had a big smile under the mask.

At the television station, Jericka parked next to a makeup trailer. I could already hear the music blasting before we entered. Inside, two ladies were in the midst of a "twerk-off," and I was quickly recruited to judge whose booty bounced best. I was laughing so hard, tears ran down my un-puffed face. Jericka turned the music off and introduced me to Bindi Wong and Sahai-Rose Wright, owners of Wright & Wong Beauty Sisters.

Bindi, a Chinese American makeup artist and skin-care specialist said, "We started our business together when we were in high school."

Sahai-Rose, an African American hairstylist whose completely shaved head highlighted her beautiful face, said, "I did hair and Bindi did the makeup for all the kids in school musicals and plays, and our work was so popular—"

"We started our business right then and there—"

"And we've been working ever since, on movies, TV, and fashion shoots."

Bindi said, "We don't compete."

"We complete—each other." They said the last phrase together as they gave a high-five and dabbed.

Bindi walked over to a mobile phone that was connected to the trailer's Bluetooth. "I love to hear the beats drop

144

when I'm doing makeup, and Sahai-Rose likes listening to audiobooks."

"So we alternate days," Sahai-Rose said, guiding me to a hairdressing chair. "Today is music day. Tomorrow is audiobook day. If you don't like either, you're welcome to put on a headset and do your own thing."

As Sahai-Rose examined my hair, Bindi used a magnifying glass to survey my skin. They both said I was in pretty good shape, skin- and hair-wise. So Bindi covered my face in a moisturizing mask, while Sahai-Rose washed and conditioned my hair. While my hair was being blow-dried, she showed me her "look-book." It was a collection of photos she took of natural hairstyles she created for her clients. "Chose the look you like best for the day, and I'll make it happen." I chose the style with rows of braids from the front of my head to my signature Afro puff at the top. Sahai-Rose and Bindi worked so well together, and they were so calm, funny, and nice, I knew they'd be a great addition to Team Mango.

On our way across the parking lot to the television studio where *Top of the Morning* was produced, I asked Jericka if she'd contacted Bob and Larry and if they were available. She was kind of vague when she said, "I'll circle back when I have something concrete to tell you."

Sunny Chase, the morning show's entertainment reporter greeted us in the green room. She was very mellow and spoke in such a whispery voice that I could barely hear her. "Hi, I'm

Sunny, and I'll be interviewing you on air in about fifteen minutes." Jericka introduced me and told Sunny that she and I had reviewed the questions and were ready to go. Sunny gave a thumbs-up, complimented my outfit, whispered, "See you on the air!" and scooted out of the green room.

Fifteen minutes later, I was on the set seated on a couch that looked really soft, but in reality felt like I was sitting on a wooden bench. Sunny sat in a chair next to the couch. There were three cameras pointed in our direction, and the lights were almost blindingly bright, so I couldn't see the woman who said, "And we're live in five, four, three, two . . ."

Suddenly, Sunny Chase was vibrant and animated. "Top of the Day L.A.! I know you've all been following the Cinderella story of the little girl who made her big debut at the Hollywood Bowl earlier this week. Mango Delight, and yes, that's her real name, was so spectacular that Chrysalis Studios has signed her in a major deal to star in her own television show!" She turned to me. "Top of the day, Mango Delight! Now tell me and the rest of our early bird *Top of the Day L.A.* viewers what's it like to be the star of your own television show?"

The lights were so bright, and Sunny's teeth were ultra-white, and there were three television monitors next to the cameras on the set. On one monitor, I could see a wide shot of Sunny and me, another had a close-up of Sunny, and the other one had a close-up of me. I couldn't stop staring at the close-up of myself staring back at me. Seconds dripped by. Sunny repeated the question, "What's it like to be the star of your own television show?"

I didn't know how to answer the question. I hadn't even started working on the show yet. How would I know what it was like? I said, "Um, . . . nice?"

The rest of the interview went downhill from there. Sunny kept the smile stretched across her face asking questions that I gave one-word answers to, maybe two words if you counted, "um . . " as a word. I was sweating under the hot lights for what seemed like an hour, but in reality, it was only seven minutes when the woman in the dark called, "Cut!"

Sunny stood, patted me on the shoulder, and said, "Work a lot harder, and you'll do better. When you do your homework, you look good and make me look good, too."

Jericka led me across the parking lot back to my makeup trailer. "Don't worry about it, Mango. That was your first try; you'll get better. Besides, I bet only a few old dinosaurs are up watching this creaky local morning show anyway." Then her phone rang. When she answered it, I could hear Max yelling on the line. I guess he was one of the *few old dinosaurs*. Jericka hurried me into the trailer as she walked away briskly, trying to calm Max and assure him that I'd get better.

Bindi and Sahai-Rose had watched on the TV in the trailer. They were sympathetic and kind. They told me stories about stars they'd worked with who had done far worse on their first live interviews. Bindi said, "Remember Gabriel Faust's first time being interviewed on live TV?"

Sahai-Rose laughed. "Oh my goodness, I forgot all about that. Poor little thing was about six or seven years old and got nervous gas before going on camera. He made loud farts all the way through the interview. Practically cleared out the studio with all the funk."

I tried to laugh along, but it was half-hearted. Gabriel Faust had only been a little kid when he messed up. Here I was, nearly thirteen, and I froze like a deer in headlights. I was relieved that it was a local show, and none of my friends back home would see it. But what about Mom? I knew she'd be watching. And Symphony and Kashara; they'd surely be checking out the show and finding out that I was going to be the star of my own series, while seeing me just staring into the camera, drooling like the village idiot. And what about Eyebrows? If he saw it, he'd probably take back the contract offer.

Sahai-Rose and Bindi kept coming up with more stories about famous people they'd worked with who'd had bad first-time experiences. I appreciated that they were being sweet to me, but all the sweetness in the world couldn't wipe away my sense of failure and humiliation.

CHAPTER TWENTY-TWO

Rising from the Ashes

Jericka, Bindi, Sahai-Rose, and I had a team breakfast in the commissary at Chrysalis Studio. I didn't eat much because I still hadn't gotten over my *Top of the Morning L.A.* disaster. I kind of relaxed when Jericka suggested we play the Interview Game. The three of them would ask rapid-fire questions one after the other, and I had to answer in at least one sentence. It was fun, because they asked silly questions like "If you were a dog, what kind of dog would you be?" "If your hair were long enough to reach the moon, how much would it weigh?" "Would you rather eat foods with absolutely no seasoning or only jalapeño pizzas for the rest of your life?"

After breakfast, we went back to Conference Room A, where my first meeting with Eyebrows had taken place. This was where we'd hold a press junket. There was one camera set up with a satellite feed, so reporters from all over the country could ask me questions and then edit it to look like we were in the same room. The reporters could see me, but I could only hear them.

I changed my outfit and had my hair and makeup refreshed, and the interviews began. One by one, reporters from across the country asked me questions for five minutes, and then the satellite feed would be switched to a different reporter. I decided to pretend we were still playing the Interview Game—that made it fun. This went on for about three hours, with breaks in between interviews so I could use the restroom, have a drink and a snack, change clothes, and get touch-ups by my team.

When the press junket was finished, I had to change outfits to take a photo with E.B., where I pretended to sign a contract. It was all pretend, because as minor I wasn't allowed to sign a contract. My parents had to do that. This photo was only for publicity. Just before E.B. arrived, I promised Jericka I wouldn't call him "Eyebrows" again. I was seated at the head of the conference table, and the fake contract and a pen were handed to me. E.B. came in along with the line of "goslings" who seemed to follow him everywhere.

E.B. shook my hand. "Congratulations, young lady, we expect big things from you."

"Thank you, Mr. . . . um. Excuse, but what does E.B. stand for?"

"Why do you want to know?"

"Because I don't want to make a mistake and call you Eyebrows again."

"Well, I never tell anyone what my initials stand for. I went through a lot of teasing about my name growing up, so I keep it to myself."

"I feel you. With a name like Mango Delight, I've been teased about my name a lot, too. Mange-grow, Lame-o the fright, Brain-go Uptight. And now, since I'm gonna be on TV, the whole world is gonna have a chance to make fun of my name."

He nodded, smiled, and moved a little closer. "This is between you and me." He gestured to make his entourage back away, and whispered, "My parents named me after the holiday when they met for the first time, Easter. Our last name was Bunnington. Can you imagine the teasing I suffered growing up with a name like Easter Bunnington?"

"Oh no, you poor thing."

"So you can understand why I prefer E.B., right?"

"Sure do."

"But from now on you, and only you, can call me Eyebrows."

"And you, and only you, can call me Brain-go."

We shook hands again and posed for the cameras as I pretended to sign my contract, but I didn't have to fake a smile. Eyebrows *was* nice. Even though he seemed cold and intimidating on the outside, on the inside he had feelings, just like I did. All that coldness was to protect his sensitive side. On his way out, followed by his goslings, I called out, "See ya later, Eyebrows!"

He yelled over his shoulder, "Not if I see you first, Brain-go!"

I laughed, because the Big Bad Boss was human after all. Jericka came toward me with a stunned expression on her face. "What was that all about?"

"Eyebrows and I made a deal. We're exclusive nickname friends. Since we've been teased about our names all our lives, we decided we have to right to make fun of ourselves, but only with each other."

"Did E.B. tell you what his initials stand for?"

"Yeah."

"Really? That's one of the biggest secrets in Hollywood." She leaned in. "So, . . . what do his initials stand for?"

I drew two fingers across my lips, zipping them shut. "I'll never tell."

I fell asleep in the car on the way to the *Entertainment America* interview. I needed to rest and be on top of my game for this one. *Entertainment America* was broadcast internationally, and I didn't want to be caught speechless and drooling again.

Bindi and Sahai-Rose met us at the studio with the makeup trailer. Before I changed into my last outfit for the day, Team Mango redid my hair and makeup completely. This international interview was a big deal, and they wanted me to look my best.

In the studio I met Carlos Regalo, the host with the deepest dimples imaginable. He had been named Handsomest Man in the World by *Folks* magazine twice! So, I was a little nervous when Carlos Regalo came over to welcome me. I had watched him on TV a million times, and here I was, shaking his hand, seeing the most recognizable dimples in the world up close. There was a rumor that his dimples were insured for a billion dollars at Lloyd's of London. Up close, I could see why. "Welcome, Mango, I'm very happy to meet you."

He was so handsome, I had butterflies in my throat. "I'm happy to meet me . . . I mean, happy to meet *you*, too."

"I'm a fan. I was covering the Destiny Manaconda show at the Hollywood Bowl, so I saw you sing that night. Great job."

"Thank you, Mr. Regalo."

"Call me Carlos."

"Okay, Carlos." I couldn't control myself, I burst out in giggles like someone was tickling me!

Carlos took my hand and walked me to the set. It was the same place where I'd seen him interview the biggest stars in the world. I sat in the chair facing him, and I started to get nervous, because my buns were sitting on the same cushion where Beyoncé's buns had sat. I was about to do an interview that would be seen all around the world. Me. Mango Delight Fuller. Why me? I wasn't famous yet. Why had the Duke of Dimples, the Handsomest Man in the World—twice—wanted to interview me?

Carlos could tell my deer-in-headlights nerves were building up, because he said, "Listen, I saw the interview you did this morning. To be frank, it was pretty bad, but you know you can do a lot better. Right?"

"Yes. I've been practicing all day."

"Fantastic. And trust me, don't worry about messing up or not having an answer right away, because this interview will be on tape. We can stop and do a retake or just cut around any mistakes you might make. So, cálmate, amiga, sí?"

I said, "Sí." Someone in the dark called "action!" and we just started talking. This time the interview went uber-fast. We didn't have to cut or do any retakes. I was comfortable enough to answer all the questions fully and even make Carlos laugh at my answers a few of times. He was gushing with compliments as he escorted me back to Jericka in the green room.

Jericka stood when we walked in, and Carlos said, "This young lady is a winner and a fast learner." I thanked him. Carlos gave Jericka a hug and said, "I'm cooking ropa vieja tonight, don't be late," and left the room.

I turned to Jericka. "What did he mean by that?"

"Oh, it's nothing . . ."

"Jericka! Is Carlos Regalo your boyfriend?"

Jericka blushed. "We've been dating for a little over a year, yes."

OMGZ, this was huge! My manager was dating the hottest, most popular guy on TV! No wonder he agreed to interview me, the least famous person who ever appeared on his couch! "Wait until I tell my friend Izzy; she's gonna freak out!"

"Mango, Carlos and I do our best to keep our private lives private, so . . ."

"Oh. Okay. I understand. My lips are zipped."

"Promise?"

"Promise!" Oh boy, I felt like I'd been zipping my lips all day. Even though these juicy secrets were piling up, I had to be responsible and keep my word. Maybe I needed to move from zipping my lips to welding them shut.

On our way to the car, Jericka said, "We only have one more meeting on the schedule today."

"I thought this interview was the last thing."

"I know, but this one last thing is something I think you're going to like."

I was really tired as Jericka drove back to the Valley Arms. I wanted to fall asleep, but curiosity about the surprise kept me awake. At the hotel, Jericka went with me to our suite. What could be a surprise there? Had Dada returned earlier than expected? How could he have driven our car across country that fast?

When I knocked, Mom opened the door shouting, "Surprise!" There on the couch with big smiles on their faces were Bob Levy and Larry Ramsey, my two favorite teachers in the world!

CHAPTER TWENTY-THREE

Mango All the Time!

Once Bob and Larry arrived, Team Mango was in full effect. The studio assigned us a classroom on the back lot where Bob would coach TJ and me on our acting. Larry would teach us the songs for each episode, and he and Bob would also write new songs and submit them to Dionne for approval to use in the series.

Dionne revised and reimagined the show around me. I was to play Mango, a character who shared my name and was a lot like me but *not me*. TJ played my next-door neighbor and best friend, Taro Jones. And, drum roll, please, . . . Kashara played TJ's sister, Asha, and Symphony played Piper, Asha's best friend. We were all members of a neighborhood garage band where I sang lead. We also played a lot of funny different characters who appeared when "Mango" time-traveled.

It was a lot to wrap my head around. I'd be playing not only Mango, but people from the past or future in every episode. Bob had us do improvisation games to practice using our voices and bodies to create different characters. I was surprised how much fun it was "playing pretend" the way we used to when we were little kids. Kashara and Symphony were pros at these games, but TJ and I caught on quickly, and we all looked forward to our sessions with Bob.

Our tutor was the last member to join Team Mango. Her name was Mrs. Joyce Bush. She had blue-tinted hair and a cushiony body that came in handy when she gave one of her great hugs. She had been Jericka's favorite teacher in high school, where she had taught home economics, math, and social studies. She was retired, but took us on as a favor to Jericka and Max. "I'm too old to be taking another full-time job. It's time for me to sit back and enjoy baking in my own kitchen. Since I'll only be here for a few weeks while things get settled, you all can call me Aunt Joyce; that'll make me feel less like a tutor and more like family."

TJ, Symphony, Kashara, and I all fell in love with Aunt Joyce. She was no-nonsense about our schoolwork. Since we were all pretty much in the same grade, we took our classes in the "school trailer" and did a lot of studying together. She made time to work one-on-one with each of us during our two hours of mandatory tutoring each school day. None of us wanted her to retire, and I'm not ashamed to say, every time they brought someone in to try out as a permanent tutor, we'd find subtle ways to sabotage the replacement, because we grew to love Aunt Joyce so much.

. . .

After four weeks of pre-production, we had our first read-through on the soundstage where our sets had been built. Dionne made a big announcement before the script was handed out. "Welcome everyone to the first table-read of season one of our new series, *Mango All the Time*."

This was the first I'd heard the title of the show, and I was a little confused. I wasn't sure I liked the it, just like I wasn't sure I liked my character having the same name as I did. TJ, Kashara, and Symphony's characters didn't share their names. Wouldn't people start confusing my character with me if we shared the same name?

Bob assured me it was a good move. "Lucille Ball always played characters named Lucy on television, and it worked for her career." That was true, and I enjoyed watching *I Love Lucy*, especially with Dada, who'd seen the shows hundreds of times but always seemed to laugh at Lucy's crazy antics like it was the first time.

But *Mango All the Time*, that was the name of the show? It felt weird, and not only to me. Kashara scrunched up her nose like she'd smelled a parade of skunks and said, "Why *Mango All the Time*? What does it mean? I don't get it."

Dionne explained, "Mango is a time-traveler. She travels to the past and the future . . . all through time, all the time."

Kashara smiled. "Oh, I get it now! That's cute!" There was a hubbub of approval all around the table. I still wasn't sure how I felt about it, but what could I do? Dionne was the creator and the show runner—the boss of the show. She'd probably cleared it with Eyebrows and the rest of the studio before the announcement. When they passed around the first script, *Mango All the Time* was printed in huge letters on the cover, so it seemed to me the title was a done deal.

The table-read went well. My character, Mango, had a lot of similarities to me (we liked the same foods, colors, music, and so on), but she was way funnier and more daring than I ever was. Dionne was an excellent writer; no wonder she got to create her own show! At the end of the table-read, we were all excited about shooting our very first *Mango All the Time* episode in a few days.

Mom and Dada (who'd returned to L.A. exhausted after packing our essentials at home and driving cross-country in our family car) missed the first read-through because it was also moving day. They were busy loading the boxes Dada had sent from home into a truck and driving to Destiny's house on Sunset Plaza Drive in the West Hollywood hills, where we'd be living for at least the next six months.

I had suggested Mom and Dada take Destiny's room, because it was super large, had a great view, and I thought they should have the best room because they were my parents. But Mom had other ideas. There was an equally large suite downstairs that was connected to a smaller room next door. Mom decided those rooms would be ideal, because Jasper would be close to her and Dada.

For the first few days it seemed like we were all walking around on eggshells because we weren't used to living in such large, fancy surroundings. Mom was almost freaked out the day the gardeners showed up unannounced. She hid in the pantry because she had no idea who they were, until they started mowing and raking and watering the grounds. She was equally surprised the morning Gloria and her house-keeping crew arrived bright and early and entered by using the secret code that unlocked all the doors. Mom, Jasper, and I retreated to the backyard while they cleaned. Mom said, "I wish I'd known they were coming this morning. I would've straightened up the house."

"Why, Mom? That's their job."

"I know, and I'm glad they're here. It would take me a month of Sundays to clean this place by myself. But still, I don't want them thinking we're slobs. Next time I'll know when to expect them and straighten up the place before they arrive."

Dada was having a fine time in the indoor and outdoor kitchens. The appliances were all top of the line and prac-tically brand new since Destiny never cooked. "You know, Mango-gal," Dada said, laughing as he was preparing dinner one night, "a man could get used to all this luxury and ele-gance in the kitchen. I hope me don't get spoiled to the point me can't cook nowhere else!"

The night before shooting the first episode, I slept off and on, waking up every hour or so and going over my lines and blocking. I wanted to be letter-perfect. I wanted to make Mom and Dada and Jericka and Max and even Eyebrows proud. Since the table-read, Dionne and Bob had taken us through lots of rehearsals with the cameras. and we'd spent hours learning and recording the song for the week and getting familiar with the sets. I was ready, but still . . . I had a lot of fears and doubts about myself, and as hard as I tried to push them out of my mind, I couldn't make them go away.

It was audiobook day in the hair and makeup trailer, which was a relief. I loved the music Bindi played, but on this day it would have made me even more nervous to have everyone jumping around, dancing and singing. Sahai-Rose had chosen to play *Kindred*, a science fiction novel by Octavia E. Butler. *Kindred* was about a Black woman named Dana who traveled through time from her home in L.A. back to a plantation in the antebellum South, where she and her ancestors were enslaved. We had been listening to the book every other day I was in the trailer for hair and makeup tests, and I was intrigued by the story. Was it because my character was a time traveler? Was it also because as a Black girl, it made me think about how far we had come as a people and how scary it would be for a girl like me to travel back to a time before the Civil War? I wondered if we'd ever do a story like that on *Mango All the Time*.

All dressed and ready to tape the first episode, I could hear the audience loading into the studio. I knew it would be made up of groups of middle grade and high school students because they were the target audience of the show. There were about three hundred seats in the studio. Three hundred of my peers would be watching me. Judging me. Would they laugh and enjoy the show the way we wanted them to? Would they boo? My hands began to shake uncontrollably.

I was sitting in front of the mirror, clenching and unclenching my fists to try to get my hands to stop shaking when Mom came into my dressing room. She told me Dada and Jasper were in the audience and were all rooting for me. Then she noticed my hands.

"What are you doing that for?" she asked.

"My hands won't stop shaking, Mom. I don't know if I can do this."

"You've had a lot of rehearsals. I know you know all your lines, because I hear you going over them around the house all the time. You're ready, aren't you?"

I sighed. "Yes, I'm ready. But being ready doesn't mean I'm not afraid. What if I mess up? What if I freeze up? What if . . ."

"What if you succeed? *Hmm*? What if you take all those feelings of fear and doubt running around in your head and make an exchange?"

"An exchange?"

"Yeah. Pretend your feelings are in a bank. And you can go to the bank and exchange your feelings of fear and doubt for feelings of excitement and energy. Those feelings are just the other side of the coin. So exchange them. Think of how exciting it is that you get to be the star of a television show. How many times have you dreamt of being right where you are at this very minute, Mango? How many kids would wish to be in your shoes right now, huh?"

Time sort of bent for a few seconds. Mom was still talking, but my mind and thoughts were flying away. Flying back home . . . I thought about Izzy and all my dramanerd friends at Trueheart Middle School. They were all rooting for me and probably wished they could be doing what I was about to do right now. Then I thought about *Kindred*. I thought about Dana going back through time to meet her enslaved ancestors. In my mind, I flew back in time, thinking about my ancestors, who may have been enslaved. I thought about them dreaming about a girl like me, far in the future, being free and having opportunities beyond their imagination.

Mom was still talking to me as I returned to the present. "Grab onto that excitement and let it energize you, baby." I hugged Mom tightly. She knew just what to say to give me the courage to step toward my future with energy and excitement.

When we were called to the set, TJ, Kashara, Symphony, and I gave each other big hugs and took our places. The first scene was set in the garage where our band rehearsed. Dionne, who was directing, called, "Action!" We sang and played our first song and got it perfect on the first take. The audience hooted, clapped, stomped their feet, laughed, and cheered throughout every scene. They gave us a standing ovation at the end of the show. We were a hit!

CHAPTER TWENTY-FOUR

All Work and No Play . . .

O nce the first *Mango All the Time* was "in the can" as they say, my life fell into a pattern that quickly became comforting but also exhausting.

> MONDAY: table-read of the new script. Hair, makeup, wardrobe meetings for the different characters we'd be playing each week in the time-travel scenes. Tutoring with Aunt Joyce, who always bought freshly made baked goods from her kitchen at the beginning of the week. Choreography if that week's episode included a dance number.

> TUESDAY: Rehearsal with Dionne or one of the other directors for the week. Costume fittings. Hair and makeup tests. Tutoring. Recording studio session for new song. Vocal and acting coaching.

WEDNESDAY: Tutoring. Location shooting for scenes
taking place outside the studio (usually on a
back lot or other location around Hollywood).
Vocal and acting coaching.

THURSDAY: Camera blocking (making sure all four
cameras were exactly where they needed to
be to get the shots necessary during the live
performance). Final wardrobe fittings. Tutoring.
Run-throughs with script memorized.

FRIDAY: Shooting day in front of a live studio
audience! I looked forward to shooting day
because it felt like we were doing a play, and
the audiences were great! After we finished
shooting the episode, we'd gather just outside
the studio when most of the audiences were
being loaded onto buses back to school. We
signed autographs, posed for pictures, and
answered questions, most of which were about
what it was like to be us.

Before leaving the studio, we'd be given a draft of the next
week's script to read over the weekend. We were on call
on Saturdays, just in case there was something we missed
during the shoot or something that needed to be added or
reshot. But Dionne went out of her way to make sure that

165

didn't happen often. She wanted us to have time to rest and recuperate for the next week. At least, that was the plan for everyone except me, the star.

There were very few Saturdays when I was completely off duty. The studio publicity department would arrange all sorts of things for me to do on my so-called time off. Some of them were fun, like attending a movie premiere, visiting children's hospitals and reading to kids, or making an appearance at an awards show. The Nickelodeon Kids' Choice Awards was a lot of fun, until I got slimed! I'd always loved watching my favorite stars get slimed, but that was before it happened to me. It took the rest of the weekend getting that stuff out of my hair, ears, nose, and the taste of it out of my mouth!

Going to store openings and ribbon-cutting ceremonies could be really tedious. I'd have to get all dressed up, then listen to a lot of speeches before getting my picture taken cutting a ribbon or something with the mayor, council member, or owner of the business. I didn't understand why I had to do this since I wasn't famous yet, but Jericka explained, "It's about getting your name out there, Mango, so when the show premieres in a few months, people will know who you are and tune in. We're building a strong foundation of recognition so the show will be a hit right off the bat."

I made it my business to keep in touch with my friends back home. Izzy and Hailey Joanne understood how busy I was, so we made an appointment for at least one catch-up group Face2Face every Sunday afternoon. I would tell them about the funny or weird things that happened at the studio, and they would fill me in on everything going on back at Trueheart Middle School.

I was shocked—no, that's not a good enough word—I was HORRIFIED to find out the new drama teacher was Zippy Levy, Bob's sister! The one who was supposed to be my escort to and from rehearsal in New York. The one who accused me of lying to her about Gabriel Faust. The one who abandoned me on the subway! I couldn't believe it. But Zippy did say she was going to give up show business and become a civilian if *Yo, Romeo!* didn't make her a star. Seems like she kept her word on that account. Still, the fact that she was teaching my friends was just astounding.

Izzy said, "I know she was horrible to you in New York, but she's a really fun teacher. She cracks a lot of jokes and hangs out with us during lunch. She's pushing for the school to let us do *Legally Blonde, the Musical* this year, and she promised me the role of Elle, you know, the Reese Witherspoon star role," Izzy gushed. "Zippy always says, 'You know, you remind me of me when I started out, kid.' Isn't that cool, a real New York professional actress said I reminded her of herself!"

I tried to sound enthusiastic. "Oh yeah, that's great Izzy," but I still didn't trust Zippy. Hailey Joanne said, "Guess who's going to be designing the costumes for *Legally Blonde*? C'est moi!"

"You? How come? You never worked on the musical before."

"This show is special. I saw it when it was on Broadway, and the costumes were incredible. *Legally Blonde* is not a show with drab old costumes designed to make the characters look like regular people; my costumes will be ultramodern. Elle dresses in couture, and who knows that better than moi?"

I had a feeling Hailey Joanne had forgotten the word "me," the way she was saying "moi" all the time. I also suspected that she and Izzy were getting closer and closer. They didn't argue on our Face2Face sessions the way they used to. In fact, they were hanging out together after school, finishing each other's sentences, and laughing at inside jokes that I was outside of. Their new closeness made me feel isolated and lonely, which was familiar, because I was feeling the same way at the studio.

When the rehearsal day wrapped for TJ, Kashara, and Symphony, they'd get to go home, while I'd need to either record lead vocals, have more costume fittings, or do interviews. It seemed like there was always more for me to do outside the studio. My castmates would sometimes get together and have pizza and movie nights or hang out at the pool at the Valley Arms or TJ's house, things I couldn't do because I was so busy all the time.

On our Thanksgiving break, I decided to do something fun with the cast so I could feel a part of the group. I invited TJ, Kashara, and Symphony over to Destiny's house for a pool party. Dada and I prepared lots of fun foods and his famous blueberry soda. I had music playing and board games all ready for a good time.

Only thing was, the three of them were in a friendship relay race that left me far behind. Lounging in the pool they shared jokes and memories, and I'd have to keep asking, "What are you talking about? When did that happen? What was that about?" Symphony and Kashara had already heard all about what happened when TJ flew home for his mother's wedding. I hadn't had the time or the chance to talk to him about it at all.

My pool party only made me feel more isolated from the cast, and especially TJ. We didn't even talk about being boyfriend and girlfriend anymore. I still *like-liked* him, but I couldn't tell if he felt the same way about me. His dad had asked him to stay in L.A. even after the show finished filming. TJ was happy about it. When he talked about how excited he was to be living with his dad full time, he never brought up the fact that we'd be on different coasts when I went back home.

One night, I was at the recording studio laying down the vocals for a song in the show. The others didn't have to come to the recording sessions because they didn't really sing or play instruments on the show (yes, TJ played guitar and sang in real life, but on the show his character was the drummer). Anyway, feedback on *Mango All the Time* from the studio was very positive, so Eyebrows ordered an album of songs from the show, to be released soon after we premiered. The idea of putting out an album was nice, but unfortunately it was another thing that made me busier than everyone else.

Anyway, while I was on a break, I scrolled through some blogs on my phone and felt a jolt of electricity go through me when I saw a photo of TJ, Symphony, Kashara, and Gabriel Faust hanging out together backstage at one of his concerts. On a Sunday night! They didn't tell me they were going. They didn't invite me. What was ten times worse, in the picture TJ was holding hands with Kashara, and Gabriel Faust had his arm around Symphony!

I was furious, but I held back my anger. I sent TJ a text politely asking him to have lunch with me the next day in my dressing room. I had to know what was going on. We had to decide, for once and for all, if we were still heading for a relationship or not!

CHAPTER TWENTY-FIVE

Crushed

My birthday was coming up, and I was at the desk in my dressing room, making a list of the people from the show I wanted to invite to the party. My birthday was the same night Felipé had scheduled Dada as guest chef at Chaos. It was a coincidence, and Dada was a little bothered by it, but I thought it would bring us both good luck. My thirteenth birthday party would be at the same place Dada got to show off his chef skills in L.A. We would share the special night together.

There was a knock at my dressing room door. It was TJ. "Hey, Mango, ready for lunch?"

"Yeah, come on in."

"Are we going to the commissary?"

"No, it's too crowded there."

"Okay. You want me to call the girls, to join us?"

"You mean Symphony and Kashara?"

He nodded. "Yeah. We have lunch together every day."

"You three do. I don't."

TJ sat on the couch, "Yeah, 'cause you're usually busy."

I felt anger rising in my chest. I couldn't believe he was playing the "busy" card. I couldn't hold back what I was feeling, so I stood up. "I wasn't busy last Sunday night when you and *the girls* went to the Gabriel Faust concert without inviting me!"

TJ's kiwi-green eyes flashed with madi-ttitude, and he stood up. "Just like you going to all those movie premieres and awards shows and never inviting the rest of us!"

"Are you kidding me?" My hands went straight to my hips, just like Mom's. "The publicity department set those events up. I don't have any say over who gets to go, that's up to them."

"Well, the publicity department set up our tickets for the Gabriel Faust show. I didn't know you wouldn't be there. If you weren't invited, that was up to them, too."

I'd had it all wrong. They weren't just hanging out on their own without me. I felt bad about jumping off at TJ like that, but still . . . "So, okay, not inviting me wasn't your fault, but . . . in the picture I saw, you're holding hands with Kashara. What's that about?"

TJ cleared his throat and sat. He looked down at his feet, sighed deeply, and ran his fingers through where his Mohawk used to be. They'd restyled TJ's hair for the show; they let the shaved sides grow and made it a more tapered faux-hawk. Finally he looked up at me, his eyes glistening,

"I don't know what to say, Mango. I mean, we haven't seen much of each other since we've been in L.A., and . . . Kashara and I just get along really well. She's nice and funny, and we like each other . . ."

On the inside, my feelings were spinning out of control. I was jealous, because the boy I *like-liked* liked another girl. On top of that, my besties back home were now more like besties with each other than they were with me. I was furious, because this was all happening because I was so busy with work. My relationships suffered because of my career. I couldn't blame TJ or Kashara or Izzy and Hailey Joanne. I was missing in action where friendships were concerned and couldn't just expect them to put their lives on hold because I had no time to share my own.

I was at a loss for words and didn't know what to say to make things better between TJ and me, so I said, "Did you know it's impossible for most people to lick their own elbows?"

TJ looked up at me curiously, then lifted his arm and tried to lick his elbow. He couldn't do it, of course. We laughed a little. He got up, came toward me, and we hugged. TJ whispered in my ear, "Friends forever?"

"Forever plus the day after that."

When he left my dressing room, I couldn't help it, I cried a little.

The night sky was filled with stars, and a cool breeze blew across the Hollywood Hills from the Pacific. We were having dinner on the patio. Usually I'd be a chatterbox filling them in on what went on at the studio that day, but on this night it was as though I'd taken a vow of silence. Mom and Dada and even Jasper noticed. Mom said, "Cat got your tongue?"

"Huh?"

"You haven't said a word since we sat down."

"And you keep pushing that crab cake from side to side on your plate," Dada said. "I made that from fresh crab I bought in Santa Monica today. It's one of the recipes I'm trying out for your party. I guess it's a big no from you."

"It's not the crab cake, Dada. It's really good, I promise." What I was feeling sad about was personal, but I had to talk about it with someone. I couldn't reach Izzy or Hailey Joanne, so I just blurted it out. "TJ and I broke up today."

"Broke up?" Mom said. "Since when were you together?"

"We weren't really together, Mom."

"You had to be together if you broke up."

Dada wagged a finger at Mom. "There ain't no *together* with nobody around here, Margie. At least not for another four or five or fifteen years!"

"Will you two chill?"

Mom said, "Who are you telling to chill?"

Dada said, "Yeah, who are you tellin' to chill?"

Then Jasper said, "Yah, who you tewwin' to shew-out?"

We all turned to my little brother and laughed and laughed. Jasper clapped and bounced in his chair. He was a showstopper and a welcome one.

Once our laughter subsided, I explained to my parents that TJ and I were just friends who were hoping to be more someday. But now he was interested in Kashara, and it was my fault.

Mom said, "It's not your fault, honey. It's nobody's fault. Things happen. Circumstances can cause feelings to change."

"That's right," Dada said, "Remember that swole-head boy you thought you were in love with, Margie, before ya Jamaican sensation came along?"

Mom giggled and waved Dada off, "Oh, please, you still bringing up Herman after all these years?"

"Herman! You still remember his name?" Dada turned to me. "Can you believe your mother was considering marrying a man named HERMAN when ME was *her man* all along!"

Jasper started banging his spoon on the table chanting, "Ha man! Ha man! Ha man!"

We laughed, and I spent the rest of the evening listening to my parents trading stories about young love gone wrong. They had both made mistakes. They both had thought they'd lost the love of their life many times, growing up. Both mourned and grieved relationships that only prepared them for the one they were truly meant to have—with each other.

I blacked out the windows in my bedroom and fell asleep releasing my first crush from my heart. Not blaming him, not blaming myself, just chalking it up to life and opening my heart to whatever or whomever came next.

CHAPTER TWENTY-SIX

Tween

M y birthday fell on a Saturday, and Dionne made sure there was no work for any of us that day. I slept in until almost eleven, but Dada was up before dawn and off to prepare for his big night. As I was yawning and stretching, Jasper burst into my room and leapt onto the bed shouting what sounded like "Hop buttday! Hop buttday!"

I hugged and squeezed him as tightly as I could before he wiggled out of my arms so he could breathe. Mom came in and took Jasper's place in my arms, saying, "Happy birthday, baby! Thirteen! Oh my goodness, where did the time go?"

We lay back on the bed, our arms still around each other. Mom's locs spread out across my pillow, the coconut scent soothing me. Jasper squirmed in between us for a group hug.

"I remember bringing you home from the hospital. Your dad and I were so nervous. He couldn't get the backward-facing car seat to fit right, and I refused to get in the car until it fit perfectly. Finally one of the nurses who'd been a mother a few times came out and hooked the car seat up properly. We drove home, your father driving as slow as a turtle.

"Who would have believed the little bundle facing backward in the car seat would bring our family so far forward before her thirteenth birthday."

"Aw, Mom . . ."

"I mean it, honey. You and your talent have changed all our lives for the better. . . . Except for one thing."

I sat up. "What one thing?"

"I miss working."

"You do? I thought you'd like being able to stay at home with Jasper."

"I love being able to do that, but Mango, I wasn't built to be a lady of leisure. I need something to do. And I don't want to be living off you. I have to contribute to our family, too."

I knew we wouldn't be living in Destiny's huge house in L.A. forever. I thought we'd just go back home once taping the show was over. I'd go back to school, Dada would start Delicious Delights catering company again, and Mom would go back to her job at Target. They'd been nice about giving her a leave of absence and assured her that her position would be waiting for her when we got back home. I said, "I'm sorry, Mom, I didn't know you were unhappy."

"Mango, I'm not unhappy, I'm just at loose ends. People come in to clean the house and take care of the garden, Sid cooks. The only thing left for me to do is look after Jasper, and he gets more independent each day. But going back to

Target now wouldn't make sense, because who'd look after your brother?"

Jasper grabbed the remote and pushed the buttons that blacked out the windows off and on, his favorite thing to do in my room. Mom took the remote away from him. "Anyway, Jericka came up with an idea I want to run by you."

"An idea?"

"Yes, see I need something that I can do at here in the house and keep an eye on this li'l munchkin at the same time."

"Uh-huh."

"Well . . ." Mom rubbed her hands together like she was nervous about something. "Jericka was looking to hire someone to start your fan club, file your press clippings, keep your website up to date, and a hundred little things like that, so she asked me if it would be a job I'd be interested in doing—"

"Hey, that's a great idea!"

"You think so?"

"Yeah! You'd be like my personal assistant!"

"Excuse me? I'm your mother, today, tomorrow, and forever. I'll be working for Jericka, assisting her, understand?

"I understand, Mom." We hugged it out and headed to the yard to pick some oranges to juice for brunch.

I relaxed by the pool while going over the next week's script and waiting for Sahai-Rose to drop by to do my hair. She wanted to give me a special moisturizing treatment and a new hairstyle as a birthday present. All of a sudden I got back-to-back texts from Izzy and Hailey Joanne; they obviously wanted to wish me a happy birthday. I answered their Face2Face on my iPad as usual, and about twenty-five individual little squares popped up on my screen, shouting, "Surprise! Happy birthday!"

I couldn't believe it, my dramanerd friends from Trueheart Middle School were on screen: Boss Chloe, Braces Chloe, and just about everyone who'd been in *Yo, Romeo*! I was overwhelmed. Mom, who was in on the surprise, brought a cupcake with one lit candle to me out by the pool. All my friends had cupcakes with one lit candle, too. They all sang *Happy Birthday*, and we blew out the candles at the same time.

I had so much fun catching up with everybody and listening to them fill me in on the latest news. Hailey Joanne's father had paid for the rights to *Legally Blonde, the Musical*, so the school would be able to put on the show presented by Mr. Pinkney's limousine and car sales business. I couldn't help it; a part of me wished I could be back home, a regular dramanerd putting on a show with my friends.

They all avoided questions about TJ, sensing he was a sensitive subject. I was sure Izzy had filled them in on what went down, and I was grateful. Sometimes it's good to have a gossipy friend who is sensitive to protecting your feelings. We had to end the party when Sahai-Rose arrived. I was grateful for the surprise Face2Face get together. It felt reassuring. I had lots of good friends, and I wasn't as isolated as I'd been feeling lately. I was thirteen, finally! Goodbye, "w." Hello, full-fledged teenager!

Sahai-Rose was putting the finishing touches on my new hairstyle, Senegalese twists, when I heard, "Mango-tango! Mango-tango, where are you?" Voza had arrived with my outfit for the big night. He found us downstairs in the salon, unzipped a garment bag, and revealed, "A golden outfit, for the golden girl!" I gasped when I saw the jumpsuit covered in golden sequins. It reflected light and sparkled like a mirror ball in a disco. There were matching high-heeled strappy sandals and a ruby necklace with a bracelet to match.

That evening before leaving, Mom and I had a pre-birthday party with Jasper. Robyn, a trusted babysitter vetted by Jericka, arrived to take care of my baby brother while we were at the party. Voza had brought Mom an outfit, too, and we giggled about how glamorous we felt as Mom drove us to Chaos, where Dada and his debut menu were waiting.

I was feeling good. It was a nice night, and I rolled the window down and enjoyed the breeze. I looked over at Mom, sitting with her back straight, her hands at ten and two on the steering wheel. I decided to have some fun. "Now that I'm a teenager, the world is opening up for me."

"Is that so?"

"Yeah. I'll be driving soon."

"Not too soon."

"Soon enough. Will you teach me?"

She looked at me for a split second and then back at the road ahead and sighed. "Yes, I guess it better be me."

"Why do you say it like that?"

"Your father is way too relaxed to be an effective driving instructor. You see the way he drives, all leaned back with his arm over the window, bopping his head to whatever music is playing. No, you're gonna need some no-nonsense nuts-and-bolts teaching, and that's what you'll get from me for sure."

I giggled. What had I got myself into? I said, "Maybe I'll just go to a driving school."

Mom laughed, "Yeah, that might be a good idea."

We drove along in silence, but we were both smiling to ourselves. I knew this would be a night I'd never forget. But at this point, I didn't know the reason why and how the upcoming events would open my eyes and change the way I saw life forever.

CHAPTER TWENTY-SEVEN

Candy Apple

Mom and I were posing for pictures on the red carpet in front of the step and repeat outside the entrance to Chaos. There so many photographers, it felt like a movie premiere. All eyes turned away from Mom and me when a candy-apple red Rolls-Royce pulled up, and out stepped Maxwell Paige. I thought he was in Europe with Destiny, and I was surprised to see him. Max said, "I flew back for your birthday, so I could give you your present in person."

My eyes went to the Rolls-Royce. "The car! It's for me???"

"No, no, no! Not the car! Candy Apple is my favorite." He reached into the car and brought out a large box and held it toward me. "Go on, open it."

"Right here?" He nodded. The paparazzi had their cameras ready. Mom and all the bystanders were watching, so I opened the box . . . and inside was a red leather purse.

Max said, "It's your very first Burstyn bag!"

The people in the crowd around us oohed and aahed, so I guessed it was a very special gift. I mean, I'd seen lots of celebrities posing with insanely expensive purses that cost thousands of dollars, but I never understood what the big deal was. Maybe because I preferred backpacks. Anyway, I gave Max a hug and thanked him for the gift.

The paparazzi took pictures of Max and me holding my Burstyn bag in front of Candy Apple. I even had a few pictures taken sitting behind the wheel. On the way inside Chaos, I asked Jericka if she could pick me up in Candy Apple from now on. She said, "Are you kidding? Out of all seventeen of my dad's cars, Candy Apple is the one he's never let me drive." I could understand why. I mean, I wasn't a car person, but Candy Apple took my breath away.

The restaurant was packed. There was a section roped off for my birthday celebration and a table piled high with gifts. Dionne, Sahai-Rose, Bindi, Aunt Joyce, TJ, Kashara, Symphony, and even Gabriel Faust were there. Carlos Regalo was there, too, but he assured me, "I'm off duty tonight." He put his arm around Jericka's waist. "I'm just here to enjoy the celebration with my girl."

We all sat together at a big table and enjoyed Dada's incredible food. He had outdone himself, using all the fresh vegetables, fruit, and seafood L.A. had to offer, creating a menu that was unique. I was so proud of him. When all five courses had been served, Dada stepped out of the kitchen in his chef coat and hat, and the entire restaurant gave him a standing ovation.

At ten o'clock the restaurant closed, and tables were moved to make room for dancing. A DJ dropped the beats, and the real party got started. I danced with Mom, Dada, Carlos Regalo, and Gabriel Faust; and TJ, Symphony, Kashara, and I did a routine we'd learned for an episode where we played a girl group from the sixties, and the crowd went wild. I was having too much fun to worry about anything negative or sad. I was celebrating my thirteenth trip around the sun, and I was the happiest girl in the world.

Symphony and Gabriel Faust approached, holding hands. Gabriel said, "My girl, Symph, tells me your show is going well."

I smiled. "Yeah, that's what they tell me."

"Cool. You know, I'm available for a guest appearance. It'd be a favor for my girl, Symph, you know. Help boost your ratings when it premieres."

Symphony said, "Wouldn't that be great? He could play, like, Julius Caesar if we time-traveled back to Roman times you know . . ."

"Of course, I'd have to have script approval," Gabriel said. "But playing an emperor sounds like a good fit for me."

Before I could answer, one of Gabriel's songs came on. "Whoa, that's my jam! Now the party is really getting started!" He and Symphony rushed to the dance floor, and I was relieved. I didn't want to make up an excuse why I didn't ever want to work with Gabriel Faust again or explain that I had nothing to do with the scripts for the show.

It was getting late, and things began to wind down. Jericka had all the gifts loaded into our car, and everyone started heading home. A valet brought Max's Candy Apple to the curb just outside Chaos. Before getting in, Max said, "I'm very proud of you, young lady. Dionne has shared rough cuts of a few episodes, and you are terrific. A young Lucille Ball who sings! You're on your way to becoming one of my most successful clients."

My head was spinning from all the excitement, and now to hear such a high compliment from Max, I was so overwhelmed I couldn't speak. Dada nudged me. "Say something, Mango."

Max said, "She doesn't have to say anything. Her work speaks for itself. I'm heading back to Switzerland to be with Destiny tomorrow, but if there is anything I can do for you, let me know. Your wish is my command."

He was about to get into his car when I said, "I wish I could drive Candy Apple."

Max looked stumped for a minute and said, "Maybe when you're old enough to drive."

Dada said, "I'm old enough."

Max said, "You're a good driver, aren't you, Sid?"

"Never had a ticket in my life."

Max tossed Dada the key fob and said, "I must be delirious, but go ahead, drive the princess home, and I'll pick my Candy Apple up in the morning."

"Are you serious, Max?" I said. "I was only joking."

Max went around to the passenger side and opened the door. "Jump in, My Lady."

Dada slid into the driver's seat. We wanted Mom to join us, but she waited for the valet to bring our car. "Y'all go ahead and enjoy yourselves. I'm gonna take your gifts home. Can I drop you off, Max?" Max accepted the offer and joined Mom on the curb as Dada drove off.

Candy Apple's interior was all white with red stitching. The leather seats were incredibly soft and comfortable. Max's initials, MP, were in golden letters at the center of the steering wheel. As we drove off, Dada said, "I can't believe it. Me, Sidney Fuller, from Ocho Rios, Jamaica, is driving a Rolls-Royce, and I ain't a chauffeur!" We giggled, enjoying the smooth ride. I took out my phone and snapped a few pictures of Dada behind the wheel.

I couldn't believe how much my life had changed since my last birthday when we had a small celebration in our apartment. Dada had made my favorite dinner: jerk chicken pizza and a red velvet cake. I had invited Brooklyn to join us, because she was the first friend I'd made at my new school, Trueheart. She gave me a friendship bracelet–making kit, and we spent the rest of the celebration in my room making bracelets for each other and planning what we'd do on New Year's Eve. Look how far I'd come and how many things had happened in just one year! I said, "Dada, my life is like a fairy tale, isn't it?"

"Sure is, baby. Mine, too, kind of . . ."

"What do you mean?"

"Chef Felipé is opening a new restaurant in San Francisco, and he offered me the position of executive chef here at Chaos."

"Really? *OMGZ*. Was he serious? Are you going to take the job?"

"Well, that depends on how long we'll be L.A."

"But . . . would you like to do it, I mean, if we stayed here?"

He smiled and shook his head as if he'd hit the lottery and couldn't believe it. "To be offered a position as executive chef of one of the most successful restaurants in town? Next to opening my own restaurant, it's a dream come true. But . . . we'll just have to see how things turn out."

As we turned off Sunset Boulevard onto our street, Sunset Plaza Drive, and headed up the hill, Dada reached out his hand to me. I took his hand thinking to myself, *Los Angeles really is the city of dreams.*

All of a sudden, multicolored bright lights flashed in the window behind us, and we heard a loud *WOOT*! Dada and I looked at each other, perplexed, as he pulled the car over to the side of the road.

CHAPTER TWENTY-EIGHT

DWB

We had just turned onto a dark, narrow, curving section of Sunset Plaza Drive. The bright lights from the police car behind us and our own headlights were the only illumination. Dada said in a hushed, urgent voice, "Put your hands up on the dashboard, Mango, and keep them there." I did as I was told. Dada pushed the button to roll down the driver's side window, put both his hands on the top of the steering wheel, and we waited.

"What's going on? What are we waiting for?"

"The officer is probably checking the license plate. Don't worry. Stay calm."

I took deep breaths, assuring myself that everything would be okay. We'd done nothing wrong. There was nothing to worry about. Then I heard more sirens approaching. Two more police cars arrived. One car pulled up in front at an angle, blocking the road ahead. The other pulled alongside the police car behind us. All the lights flashing at once were making me dizzy. I cried out and reached for Dada!

"Keep your hands on the dashboard in plain sight, Mango!"

I put my hands high up on the dashboard. They were shaking, and my breath was coming in gasps. As hard as I tried to take deep breaths, it was no use. I was beginning to panic.

A police officer approached the driver side door. "Step out of the car, please, sir."

"What is this about, officer?"

The policeman put his hand on the firearm at his hip and unsnapped the holster. "Step out of the car, sir. Now!"

Dada looked at me. He tried to appear calm, but his furrowed brow gave him away. He said, "Stay still, Mango. Don't move." He got out of the car and put his hands up above his head. Officers from the two other police cars approached. My stomach ached. My bladder was full. My whole body began trembling, and my teeth started to chatter. I felt like a guitar string wound too tight.

"Is this your vehicle?"

"No, sir, it's—"

The officer removed handcuffs from his belt. "Hands behind your back."

"Officer, you're making a big mistake!"

"It'll be a bigger mistake if you don't comply. Hands behind your back!"

I watched as Dada did as he was told, and the officer put handcuffs on him. The officer looked into the car and asked Dada, "Who's the woman in the passenger seat?"

"That's no woman, it's my daughter. She's a kid, only thirteen. We're coming back from her birthday—"

"Step to the rear of the vehicle, sir."

"Officer, if you'd just let me explain."

"Don't make me repeat myself!"

I saw the muscles in Dada's jaw tighten as he stared the officer in the eyes. He looked at me, nodded to assure me that he was okay, and moved to the back of the car. The other officers followed closely. I wanted to get out and stand by his side or run up the hill to the safety of the house, but that was more than a mile away. I had to do something, so I slowly lowered a hand from the dashboard to my lap and picked up my phone and spoke. "Hey Siri, call Mom."

The phone rang three times, then Mom picked up. "Mango?"

"Mom, the police stopped us on the road and—"

There was a sharp rap on the passenger window. "Hands where I can see them!"

Dada shouted, "Mango!"

I froze. The too-tight guitar string was plucked, and a sour, discordant note vibrated inside of me as warm liquid spilled down my leg.

I was soaking in a tub of soapy hot water when my trembling finally stopped. Mom was rinsing my back with a sponge and speaking in soothing tones. "I'm so sorry this had to happen on your birthday, baby. So sorry."

I squeezed my eyes shut but the tears pushed out anyway, dropping down my cheeks and splashing into the bathwater. I wondered what would have happened if I hadn't reached Mom on the phone. She was just about to drop Max off at his home in Beverly Hills when she answered. What would have happened to Dada if Max hadn't been friends with the chief of police? What if Max hadn't been able to set things right with one phone call?

Dada wasn't speeding; he hadn't run through any red lights or rolled through a stop sign. We were stopped on a DWB, Driving While Black. Because he was a Black man driving an expensive car Dada was considered suspicious. I knew that kind of thing happened. I'd seen horrible stories on TV news of men who looked like my father, and women who looked like my mother being pulled over, and the situation escalating to tragedy. I'd seen and heard about things like that so many times before, but until it happens to you . . . you can't imagine how frightening it can be.

By the time I was out of the bath and in my pajamas and a robe, Jericka, Dionne, and Voza had arrived. I was so embarrassed, thinking Voza would be angry about me soiling the jumpsuit that was to be returned to the designer. But Voza wrapped me in a warm hug and said, "Oh, Mango-tango, don't worry about that silly jumpsuit. I just want to make sure you're all right."

Dada had put out coffee for the adults and hot cocoa for me. Dionne was furious. "How could they do this to a child?! This kind of harassment has got to stop!"

Jericka said, "It used to happen to Max all the time. Right, Dad?"

"That's how I got to be friends with the police chief. They'd stop me a couple of times a week because a Black man in an expensive car in Beverly Hills equals suspicious."

Voza said, "Well, Max, you need to introduce me to the police chief, because they still stop me at least once a month. I'm famous all over the world, but if I'm not on a red carpet or on TV, the first thing they see is the color of my skin."

The conversation continued, everyone recounting experiences they'd had in their expensive cars being profiled by the police. Mom said, "You don't have to be in a luxury car to get stopped. Right, Sid?"

Dada nodded. "Yeah, you're right. I was stopped in our little compact back home just last summer."

"While I was away in New York?"

"Yes. I was coming back from a catering job out there by where your friend Hailey Joanne lives. I got stopped and had to answer a barrage of questions about why I was in that particular neighborhood at night."

"Why didn't you tell me, Dada?"

"We didn't want to worry you, Mango."

"We were trying to protect you," Mom said.

"From what? From reality?" I looked at all the faces of the caring adults around me. "I'm not blind to what's going on in the world. I know what that flight attendant was thinking when she tried to stop us from boarding with the first-class passengers. I know why none of the men at that board meeting looked like any of us. It's just . . . I never thought . . . It's different when—"

"When it happens to you?"

"Yeah."

My hands started shaking again, and some of my cocoa splashed on my robe. Mom said, "Mango has had enough for tonight. I'm putting her to bed."

Dionne came over and hugged me. "You get some rest and call me if you need anything, okay? See you Monday."

Jericka said, "Call me if you need anything. Okay?"

I nodded, and Mom walked with me to my bedroom. Once in bed, I didn't use the button to black out the windows. I stared out at the rolling blanket of twinkling lights below. How had my magical dream city become a nightmare so fast?

I tried my best to stay awake, not wanting to risk dreaming about what we'd been through. But my eyes, raw from all the tears, finally gave way, and I fell into a deep and thankfully dreamless sleep.

CHAPTER TWENTY-NINE

Jackrabbit

When I woke up, the sun was streaming through the walls of glass, filling the room with light. The sky was a cloudless blue, *another beautiful L.A. day*, I thought. Then I began to remember how the night ended. The sirens. The strobe lights. The holster being unsnapped. The handcuffs. I reached for the remote control on the nightstand, pushed the button to black out the windows, burrowed under the covers, closed my eyes, and willed myself back to sleep.

Later, there was a soft knock, and my door opened. A shaft of light broke through the darkness, and Dada's silhouette filled the door frame. He came in and sat beside me on the bed. "Ready to get up and start the day, Mango-gal? I can fix you something to eat."

"I'm not hungry."

"Okay, well . . . I'm gonna go for a run; get up and come with me."

A run? Was he kidding? I hadn't done that in so long, and I had no intention of going on a run today. Yes, I used to love running. I always felt better after a good run when I was on the Girls On Track team back at Trueheart. But today? After what happened last night? I didn't want to go out of the house, much less run. I turned away from Dada and said, "No. You go ahead, Dada, I don't want to."

Dada picked up the remote and cleared the windows so that sunlight filled the room again. "I'm not giving you a choice this morning. We're going for a run. Now get up, get dressed, and let's go."

"Dada, no!" I reached for the remote to black out the windows again, but Dada, at the door, held it up in his hand. "No more darkness, Mango-gal. Time to get out in the light. Now come on!"

I dragged myself out of bed and grudgingly dressed to join Dada outside. We stretched, did Frankenstein kicks and jumping jacks, just like I used to do at track practice, and then we set off jogging up the hill. It wasn't easy, since it had been such a long time since I'd run. I would run a little, then walk, then run a little more. Dada ran backward most of the way, encouraging me, "Come on, Mango-gal! Keep those knees up. Fill up ya lungs! Move-it, move-it!"

As much as I didn't want to, I kept going. With all his nudging, Dada struck something in me. It was the thing that wouldn't let me give up, even when I wanted to. The thing in me that always had something to prove and wouldn't stop pushing me until I had done what I set out to do.

My lungs began to fill with air, expanding my back and my rib cage. I could feel blood pumping through my legs, my arms, my heart. All of a sudden I was running full out up the hill. Challenging Dada to keep up with me. The sweat pouring down my face, cooling me in the breeze, felt good. When we reached the top of Sunset Plaza Drive we stopped. Dada was breathing hard. He bent over, his hands on his knees, sucking in air. I was a little winded, but not nearly as much as he was.

There was an empty lot with no houses near the top where you could look out and see scores of homes down below. Aquamarine swimming pools sparkled in the sun alongside pastel-colored houses and swatches of vibrant green lawns and trees. We sat on the sandy hillside, looking out west across L.A., past Century City, toward Santa Monica and the Pacific Ocean. A police helicopter circled the sky in the distance. The lightness I felt began to drain from me. I guess my face showed how quickly my mood was changing, because Dada said, "Don't let the bad thoughts bring you down, Mango-gal."

I had to squint in the sunlight looking up at him, "I can't help it. I can't forget."

"I'm not asking you to forget. I'm asking you to fight back."

"How? What can I do to stop what happened last night from ever happening to us again?"

Dada was quiet for a few moments. He was gazing out over the city, but his thoughts were far, far away. Finally, he said, "When I was a wee boy of five or six, back home in Jamaica, I was jealous of my older brothers and sisters."

"Why?"

"Because my parents had given each of them a plot of land to grow their own gardens. They competed to see who could grow the best fruits and vegetables. They all worked hard, tilling the soil, planting, weeding, fighting pests that tried to destroy their crops. At harvest time each year, my parents would celebrate the sibling with the most bountiful plot. We'd have a canning competition, and the one who filled the most jars would be the winner, and he or she would get to sit at the head of the table, right beside my father.

"I wanted to sit at the head of the table so, so bad! I begged for my own plot of land to show that I could tend a garden as good as any of them. But my parents said I was too young for such a responsibility. I had to wait until I was older. That didn't sit well with an impatient jackrabbit boy like me. That was my nickname, Jackrabbit, you know, 'cause they say me could run before me could walk. And I was always in a hurry. So, my mother gave me a young potato plant in a hanging pot. It was beautiful and lush, with vibrant green leaves that hung down like a gentle waterfall. Mama say, 'Jackrabbit, if you can take care of this plant and not let it die for a whole season, we will give you your own plot. But, if the plant should die, that will show you not ready for to grow a garden of your own.'

"Me was soooo excited! I had complete confidence in myself. I knew I could do it. Each morning, me get up and water my potato plant. I watched the leaves grow longer hanging down from the pot. There was no way I could lose. But one morning, it was so very hot, the jackrabbit in me got up early and set off down the hill to the beach with my friends, where we stayed and played and had so much fun all day. I was so wrung out, when I got home, me went straight to bed. No dinner or nothin'.

"The next morning, when I woke up, I went out to the porch to water my potato plant. I was shocked, yes! All of the beautiful green leaves were drooping, shriveled, and hanging down looking dead! I had failed and because I neglected them for one day, I had lost them. I sat down on the steps under my plant and cried. Mama come outside, looked at me sitting there sniffling, and she say, 'You give up like dat? You think it all over? You think the plant there dead? You got no faith in yourself? Get up, bwoy! Grab de watering can. If you want that plant to live, make it so!' And that's what I did. I went to the pump, filled the watering can, and poured the life back into my potato plant. And let me tell you, by the afternoon, the leaves them was plump and green and flowing down again."

"That's a cool story, Dada, but what does it have to do with last night?"

"Whenever something so wrong happens to me, and my spirit is close to being broken and shriveled up, I think of my potato plant and how all it took was some water to bring it back from the edge, and I find a way to water myself."

"Water? You just drink water to feel better?"

He chuckled. "No, Mango-gal, I'm using 'water' as a metaphor for self-care. Today my water is running. Getting out in the sun and pushing myself up the hill, proving to myself that I am too strong to be beaten by whatever unfair challenges life throws in front of me. And then I set out to look at the world with clear eyes and do whatever I can to live my best life, lead by example, and strengthen my resolve to change the world."

The sweat on Dada's brow glistened as he smiled his broad, beautiful smile at me. I leaned in, and he put his arm around my shoulder. Looking out at the city below, I understood how giving in to fear and hopelessness was a defeat. I had to keep watering my spirit with hope and action. Maybe by doing that, I could effect change on the world, too.

I stood up, "Come on, Jackrabbit, race you down the hill. Last one to the house is a wilted potato plant!" Dada leapt to his feet, and off we went down the hill, around the curves, all the way back to the house. It was a close race, but I won!

CHAPTER THIRTY

Influencer

I was feeling so good when we got back home, I couldn't wait to get back to the studio and get to work on Monday. Mom said, "I'm glad you're feeling better, but take some time for yourself. Besides, you haven't even opened your birthday gifts." I'd forgotten all about the pile of presents from the party. I took a shower, changed clothes, and hurried to tackle the beautifully wrapped gifts Mom had stacked by the piano.

Jericka had arrived by the time I was ready. Mom was by her side with pen and paper and a stack of thank-you notes. It was part of Mom's new job to keep track of who gave me what and make sure their gifts were personally acknowledged.

I opened Mom and Dada's gift first. It was a framed poster from the Off-Off-Off-Broadway production of *Yo, Romeo!* signed by all the cast members! I loved it and gave them both big hugs. Next I opened a present from Aunt Zendaya. It was a lovely bracelet she made with precious stones and a real acorn charm where the bracelet latched. The card read, "Happy Birthday, Sweet 13! Love Aunt Zendaya and Acorn." My aunt and my New York stage manager were still dating. I was happy I had been the one to introduce them.

TJ gave me a boxed set of *Weirdest Facts from Around the World*! It included eight books. I was sure he'd read each and every one of them. I smiled, because I knew TJ still cared about me.

The rest of the gifts were very nice; a jeweled mango pin from Eyebrows, a locket from Dionne, fancy fountain pens for signing autographs from Kashara and Symphony, a diary from Aunt Joyce, a funny certificate for one thousand free rides around L.A. from Tabby. Then there were a lot of gifts from companies and people I'd never met or heard of. I didn't know how they even knew it was my birthday or why they would send me clothes, shoes, watches, perfumes, necklaces, and sunglasses for free.

Jericka said, "Those are promotional gifts. The companies want you to wear them when you're getting photographed or mention them on social media. You're becoming an "influencer," Mango. Girls and boys are going to want to know what you like, want to be like you, and want to dress like you."

I wasn't sure how I felt about being an influencer. I wasn't even allowed to be on social media yet. I said, "I don't want to be fake and wear something that I normally wouldn't wear just because I got it for free."

"You don't have to," Jericka said. "Keep the things you like, and we can donate whatever you don't to raise money for a worthy cause."

"Do you think people would be upset or think I was being ungrateful if they found out I didn't keep their gifts?"

"I don't think that would matter if the gifts went to a good cause. Some of them are worth a lot of money."

"How much do you think the Burstyn bag Max gave me is worth?"

"I don't *think*, I know it cost seven thousand dollars."

Mom said, "For a pocketbook? That's Californi-crazy if you ask me!"

I knew the bag was expensive, but I had no idea it would cost that much. Just because it cost a lot of money didn't make me want it more. I said, "Would Max be mad if I donated it to charity?"

"He wouldn't be upset at all, since he got it for free."

"For free? Why would anyone give away a seven thousand dollar bag for free?"

"Remember those pictures you and Max took, with you holding the bag?"

I did remember. He insisted I open his gift before we even went in to the party, so the paparazzi could take pictures of me holding it. I said, "Uh-huh."

"Those pictures will be on social media and maybe in magazines all over the world. That kind of publicity is worth much more than seven thousand dollars. Celebrities get lots of things for free, Mango, but it's a trade-off. People like to follow trends set by famous people, and that means a lot of money for companies that supply the goods. Understand?"

"Yeah, I get it now. I don't know how I feel about it, but I get it." I looked at all the gifts. Except for the ones from my friends and family, I didn't feel like I deserved them. "I think I'd like to donate these to a charity to raise money for a good cause."

"Great idea," Jericka said. "What kind of charity are you thinking of?"

"I don't know yet. I've never done anything like that before. Can I think about it?"

"Sure, take all the time you need."

I went back to my room to study my script. This week, "Mango" would travel back in time as Cleopatra, shopping for the perfect pet, an asp. It was a funny episode, but I began to wonder what it would mean for the kids watching. "Mango" had traveled into the future as a spy, a spaceship captain, a kooky inventor, and a president of the United States, but even that episode was about President Mango trying to trick the Secret Service agents (played by Kashara and Symphony) and sneak out of the White House to have a pizza date with her rock star crush (played by TJ, of course).

Then there were the episodes where "Mango" traveled back in time. She was the lead singer of a girl group from the sixties, a riverboat captain, and a damsel in distress menaced by a two-headed dragon played by Symphony and Kashara and rescued by a brave knight played by TJ. They were all fun shows to do, but I began to wonder if the stories could be more than just fun. I remembered the night of Destiny Manaconda's party when she described the show as TV fluff. I was beginning to understand what she meant and started thinking about what I could do about it.

At dinner, Dada discussed the offer from Chef Felipé and what it would mean for our family. "We'd need to stay here in Los Angeles indefinitely. We'd have to get a more affordable home, but I'd be making considerably more money. There are a lot of positives to consider."

"A lot of negative, too," Mom said. "Like what happened last night."

Dada looked at me and then back to Mom. "Let's discuss this later."

I said, "Why?"

"We don't want to upset you, Mango."

"I'm not a baby, Dada!"

Mom reached out and patted my hand. "Okay, relax. How do you feel about moving here permanently, honey?"

I immediately regretted insisting I be included in the discussion, because I didn't know how I felt about it. Before what happened with the police the night before, I was excited about the idea of staying in L.A., but now . . . We only had two more episodes of the ten *Mango All the Time* shows the studio had ordered. What then? Would I go to a regular school in L.A. or go back home to Trueheart, where I'd get to be with my friends. Then again, Dada had a great opportunity for his career right here in West Hollywood. He and Mom had sacrificed our regular lives for my career; shouldn't I be willing to do the same for Dada?

"Mango?" Dada said, "What's your opinion?"

"I don't know . . ." I slid my chair back from the table. "May I be excused, please? I'm tired, and I want to go to bed so I'm ready for work tomorrow."

"But you've hardly eaten a thing."

"Let her go, Margie. Goodnight, baby."

I kissed Mom, Dada, and Jasper and headed to my room. I blacked out the windows and lay down on the bed. My mind was racing. The party. The gifts. The officer unsnapping his holster. The sirens. The blinding lights. All these images were swirling in my head; it was like a whirlpool sucking me underwater, and I was helpless to fight it.

D

A

D

A!!!!

He'd been arrested. I arrived at the prison. It was a tall building that towered over all the buildings surrounding it. There was only one window, high above. The window had bars. I cried out, "Dada!" Then I was inside, being led down a long corridor toward a gate. The gate slid open, I entered, and it slammed shut behind me. I looked ahead, and there was another gate down a long corridor. I hurried to the gate. It slid open, I entered, and it slammed closed behind me. Ahead there was another long corridor, and another gate and another gate and another gate and another. . . .

CHAPTER THIRTY-ONE

The Talk

I was sweating when I awoke. Dada was up early, too. We talked about our dreams and how funny and scary it was that we'd both dreamt about the "incident." In his dream, the car kept getting stopped, over and over. Different cars, same police. In my dream, I was searching for him, over and over. We went for a run to clear our minds and power up for the day.

I was dressed and ready to go the studio when Jericka arrived. I'd been expecting Tabby in the van, the usual way I was picked up to go to work. But now Jericka was here in a dark red DeLorean. Another one of Max's seventeen cars. A flashy, very noticeable sports car. I felt a mango pit beginning to grow in my stomach. Dada and I had been in one of Max's fancy, expensive cars when we were pulled over two nights earlier. I tried to talk the mango pit away, make it shrink to nothing. *You're just being silly, Mango. It's daytime now. Nothing like that is going to happen again. Not ever!* I settled into the front seat next to Jericka. "Where's Tabby? Is he sick?"

"No, I just wanted to pick you up this morning to make sure you're okay."

"I'm fine. I'm not a baby."

"I didn't say you were, I just wanted to check on you."

I shrugged, buckled my seat belt, and opened my script, pretending to go over my lines. I felt bad about being so cranky. I thought the run had chilled me out. Maybe it was the nightmare and the restlessness I felt all night. I was debating if I should apologize for snapping at Jericka or not. I decided to just drop it; apologizing would make it a bigger deal than it was. We rode in silence for a long time, then Jericka said, "Carlos wants to interview you this afternoon during the lunch break for a piece about your birthday."

"Why?"

"Good publicity for the show."

"Is he going to ask me about what happened after . . . with the police?"

"No. I don't think he knows anything about that, but . . . do you want to talk about it?"

"No! I want to forget it. I don't want anybody to know about it."

"Okay, that's fine. Never mind. I'll cancel the interview."

I liked Carlos Regalo, his show was really popular, and he was probably interviewing me again as a favor to Jericka. How could I say no? "Don't cancel it, I'll do it."

I rolled my neck from side to side and took deep breaths. I tried to focus on how good I'd felt after the run. I was beginning to bring back that sense of calm, and the mango pit in my stomach was beginning to shrink when I heard the *WHOOP-WHOOP* of sirens.

Jericka pulled the car over to the side of the street, as did all the cars ahead of us. An ambulance whizzed past. By the time the sound of the whooping sirens began to fade, my heart was racing and my hands were shaking. Jericka must've noticed, because she said, "Mango, are you all right? It was just an ambulance."

"I know. I'm fine. It just startled me. Let's go." I pretended to study my script again, but my eyes kept getting watery, and it was hard to make out the words on the page. I turned my face to the window so Jericka couldn't see. I closed my eyes, took deep breaths, and concentrated on being okay. *Nothing is wrong, Mango. Come on now, it was just an ambulance. Take deep breaths. You're all right. You're fine. You're okay . . .*

We were filming an outdoor scene on the back lot that would be shown during the live audience taping on Friday. I was dressed as Cleopatra on a barge, on my way to buy a new pet. Kashara and Symphony were my ladies in waiting, arguing over what kind of pet I should buy.

"A camel would be wonderful!"

"No, they spit, and their humps make Her Majesty itch!"

"How about a hippo or a baboon or a crocodile?"

"Too huge, too stinky, too toothy!"

Things were not going smoothly, and we had to do a lot of retakes. Normally, I would have been calm and making jokes between the takes as the barge was pulled back to the starting point, or the lights were repositioned, or batteries or lenses on the camera were being replaced, but I was quiet. For some reason, I kept getting more and more irritated, especially when Kashara and Symphony laughed and made jokes about having to do another take. Finally, I snapped, "Will you all just shut up and stop playing around!" I stepped off the barge and headed for my dressing room trailer.

Bob called after me, "Mango, we're almost ready for another take."

"Call me when you're finally ready to get it right!" I stormed into my trailer and slammed the door. I sat down in front of the mirror, pulled off the crown, and sobbed. I didn't know what was wrong with me. Who was I? Why was I so agitated and mean? Nobody had done anything wrong or said anything to deserve how I'd just behaved. There was a knock at the door, "Please, go away!" More knocking. "I said, go away! Please!" Knocking continued, but this time it was like fingers thrumming on the door. That was it, enough! I went to the door and yanked it open prepared to yell, when I saw . . .

"It's just me. Don't bite my head off," TJ said.

"What are you doing here? You're not in this scene."

"I stopped by to watch. I thought it'd be funny, but, man, you really turned on the drama."

I shut the door. "TJ, I'm really not in the mood."

210

He said, "I know what happened."

I stopped and took a breath. I opened the door an inch and peered out at him. He said, "We all do." Kashara and Symphony peeked out from the side of the trailer. "Can we come in?"

I let the door open all the way, and they all came in and sat on the couch. "I'm sorry I told you to shut up and stormed off like that. I don't know what's wrong with me."

"Girl, don't worry about it," Kashara said.

"We're really sorry about what happened the other night," Symphony said. "It's not fair they treated you and your father like that just because—" She stopped herself, looked at each of us, then went on, "I mean . . . you know, because . . ."

Kashara said, "Go on and say it, we all know why the police stopped him. It was a straight-up DWB, Driving While Black!"

"I know, I just feel, I don't know, guilty."

"Why do *you* feel guilty?" I asked.

"Because," her hands fluttered and fussed with her auburn curls, "Because they wouldn't have stopped my father . . . unless he was driving a helicopter down the street or something."

Kashara rolled her eyes. "You can't drive a helicopter, Symphony."

"I know, but that's the only reason they'd stop someone who looked like my father."

"That would be because he was doing something impossible, not because of the color of his skin."

Symphony stood up, turning beet red. "That's my point!"

Kashara stood up and stepped toward her. "Well, if you're gonna make a point, at least try to make it make sense!"

"Oh yeah, what are you going to do about it?"

"Maybe I'll knock some sense into you!"

I stood and got between them. "Hold it! Stop!"

TJ was laughing so hard he had to hold his stomach. The three of us girls turned on him. "What are you laughing at?"

"Yeah, what's so funny?"

"You sound like a hyena!"

TJ finally pulled himself together enough to sputter, "Look at the three of you. Dressed in those costumes arguing about what does or doesn't make sense!"

The three of us looked at our reflections in the mirror, and we couldn't help ourselves; we laughed, too. We did look ridiculous. After we all calmed down, I apologized again. "I didn't mean to be so crabby today. I guess . . ."

"You're not over what happened," Kashara said. "My dad said you probably would need some time to get over the trauma."

"Your dad?"

"Yeah, he took some vacation time and came to visit over the weekend. He's a police officer back home in Chicago."

"I didn't know that," I said.

"Yeah. He said he hoped you wouldn't think all cops were bad. They're not. But it can be hard not blaming all police officers. Most police officers are good; some are bad apples."

"And some are racist apples." Symphony said.

Kashara said, "Symphony, that's not fair."

"Yeah, it is. What else would you call it when the only reason you get stopped is because of the color of your skin?" TJ said. "When we heard about it yesterday, my dad said it's happened to him, too. Then he gave me a long talk about what to do if the police ever stopped me. I tried to tell him my mom had given me *the talk* many times before, but he insisted and went over it all again. Keep your hands where they can be seen. Do what you're told. Don't resist. No sudden movements."

"That's what Dada was saying to me last night."

"It's nothing new," Kashara said. "My parents have said it to my brothers and me over and over again—and my dad's a police officer."

Symphony said, "No one's ever said anything like that to me. No one has ever warned me about anything having to do with the police."

"That's because the police aren't considered a threat in your world." TJ looked at Kashara and me. "It's different for us."

There was a knock at the door, and Bob entered. I thought he was going to call us back to the set, but he said, "Mango, Dionne wants to see you in her office. Tabby's waiting to give you a ride over."

Kashara said, "*Oooooh*, you're in trouble."

I believed she was right. I sighed and headed for the door, feeling bad about the way I had behaved but sort of good at the same time. I turned to my friends. "Thanks for "barging" in. Get it? Cleopatra? Barge? *BARGING IN???*" They groaned at my weak joke. "Seriously, talking with you all made me feel better. I'll be back if I don't get fired."

I left my trailer. Tabby was waiting in the golf cart. I sat next to him, trying to think of ways to apologize for my diva-zilla moment and hoping Dionne would forgive me.

CHAPTER THIRTY-TWO

The Back End

I entered Dionne's office a full apology bursting from my mouth. "I'm so sorry! I never meant to act like such a diva, but I couldn't help myself. I think I've just been irritated and kind of acting out, because of what had happened . . ."

I stopped apologizing when I realized both my parents were there, along with Jericka and my lawyer, Maria Perez-Blue, and Eyebrows, too! I must've really messed up to have all of them in Dionne's office. But it was strange—they were smiling. No, more than smiling, they were beaming, which meant their eyes were brighter than their smiles. I slowly sank down into the nearest chair. "What's going on?"

Eyebrows stood. "Well, Brain-go . . . "

Mom nudged Jericka. "What did he call her?"

"It's a thing they do," Jericka assured her. "Sort of a game."

"It's okay, Mom, he calls me Brain-go, and I call him Eyebrows."

Mom looked at Eyebrows, probably noticing how bushy his eyebrows were. She shook her head and shrugged. "Okay. Go on."

Eyebrows, who was obviously not used to being interrupted, cleared his throat and continued, "We've been doing a lot of testing of the first six episodes with audiences of several different demographics."

Mom interrupted again. "Which audiences, exactly?"

"Different age groups. We tested the episodes with kids of course, younger and older. We tested with teens, and we even did thorough testing with adults. I'm happy to say the show tested through the roof with every group. The results were a surprise and a . . . to use your middle name, Brain-go, . . . a delight."

My cheeks flushed, and my face was getting hot. Eyebrows went on, "We're confident that once the show premieres, it's going to be a huge hit, and so we've decided to go ahead and green-light the back end."

I looked at Dionne. "The back end?"

She smiled. "Thirteen more episodes, a full-season order of twenty-three."

I was stunned. I didn't know how to react. While everyone around me was "yayyy-ing" and clapping, I just sat there, no expression on my face whatsoever.

Eyebrows tried to cheer me on. "This is a big deal. Something we never do unless a big star is involved and forces our hand. But you, young lady, you're going to be a huge star. One of the biggest, I'd venture to say. We have great confidence in you, Dionne, and the show."

Mom, Dada, Jericka, and everyone were looking at me expecting some kind of reaction. I just sat there, letting it all sink in. Thirteen more episodes? I thought we were almost finished shooting the first ten. I was looking forward to being done. I was so flustered, I didn't realize I was talking out loud when I said, "What if I don't want to do more?"

Eyebrows's eyebrows lifted then scrunched together, and he sat back down. Dionne looked to Mom and Dada, who in turn looked to Maria Perez-Blue. Finally my lawyer said, "Mango the studio has an option in your contract. It's pretty standard business. They can order more episodes—and even one or two more seasons—if they like. This is a good thing. Something most actors would want to happen."

Dada said, "Mango-gal, are you unhappy?"

"No, I just . . . I guess I was expecting to be finished."

Dionne said, "You're probably worn out, I know. We're taking a three-week hiatus. You'll get some rest before we start up again."

Mom said, "That sounds good, doesn't it, honey? We can go back home, and you'll get to spend some time with your friends."

I hadn't thought of that. A chance to hang with Izzy and Hailey Joanne and my dramanerds crew would be awesome. Back at home in my own bed, back to my real life, that could be just the thing I needed to stop feeling so . . . weird. I nodded. "Yeah, that'll be fun."

As everyone was leaving Dionne's office, she asked me to stay behind for a chat. "I heard about what happened on the set earlier. What's going on?"

I sighed. "I don't know. I'm really sorry."

Dionne perched on the edge of the desk in front of me. "Do you think it had anything to do with what you went through the night before last?"

The mention of that night made my head begin to ache. I didn't want to think about it, but ever since it happened, it was always there, lurking in the back of my mind. "Maybe it did. Just a little. I mean, I'm playing Mango being Cleopatra looking for a pet asp while stuff like what happened to Dada and me is happening again and again all over. I guess I just felt a little silly, and that made me irritated and angry . . . I guess."

Dionne said, "That's only natural. What you went through was traumatic. It challenged your feelings of safety in the world. I understand that. What you have to do now is find a way to channel your energy into doing something about it. Something positive."

"How?"

"Well, I try to write about the things that affect me deeply. The idea for this show came about when I was frustrated how hard it was to break into this business as a Black woman. I had to work twice as hard to get what I knew I deserved. I used to daydream about how cool it would be if I could go back in time or into the future and make things better. My frustration was the seed of the idea that turned into this show."

"I wish I could do that."

"Who says you can't?"

"I do! I don't know how to write a TV show."

"You'll never know until you try. You get scripts every week. You know what the format is and how the show works. Wouldn't it be cool to write about what happened to you? Take that negative and turn it into something positive?"

"You mean, like a script for *Mango All the Time*?"

"Perhaps it could turn into that. Your character could travel back in time or into the future and find out why things like what happened to you happen and maybe do something about it."

"But I'm just an actor."

"*Just*? About a year ago you were just a student. Then you became a singer, an actor, and now you're a TV star. . . . Why limit yourself, Mango? Spread your wings, girl! Don't let an opportunity like this pass you by."

Something about what she was saying excited me. I felt butterflies in my stomach instead of my usual mango pit. "I guess I can try."

"Listen, while we're on hiatus, the writers and I will be preparing new scripts for when we resume production. Jot some ideas down, share them with me, and we'll see if what you come up with could be good for the show. Okay?"

"Yeah . . . Okay . . ."

I could feel the electricity in my brain sparking as I headed back to the set to continue shooting the Cleopatra scene. A zillion little baby ideas whirled through my brain while we were finishing the scene. Between setups, I dictated the ideas into my phone. Some were good. Some were awful. Still, I was more excited than scared, more hopeful than discouraged. If I could make something positive out of what happened to Dada and me, maybe it would turn what had ruined my birthday into something that could change the world!

CHAPTER THIRTY-THREE

Alien

O kay, maybe I was being a little optimistic about changing the world, but why just reach for the moon when you can aim for the stars? Finishing the last two of the first ten episodes of *Mango All the Time* before the break seemed to go really fast. Everyone in the cast and crew was happy we would get to do more shows and that the studio thought we'd be a hit, but having a three-week hiatus (TV talk for a break) made us even happier.

Symphony and Kashara couldn't wait to get back to their friends and family, just like me. TJ was going to stay in L.A. for the time being, since his mother was still on her honeymoon. I was happy I'd get to sleep in my own bed, hang out with my besties, and just be regular old Mango again.

My family and I took a late Saturday night flight back home. I was so excited, there was an ache in my belly that was more than homesickness. I was home hungry. Hungry to get back to my friends. Back to my own room. Back to my own bed. Back to the me I was before all the wonderful and not-so-wonderful things happened to me. I knew I was lucky and that a lot of kids would think my life was a dream. Looking from the outside, I could understand that, because that's what I believed, too. All the years of idolizing Beyoncé and Destiny Manaconda, I never realized how much hard work and sacrifice went into making everything they did look glamorous and easy.

Mom, Dada, Jasper, and most of the people on the plane were sleeping peacefully in the darkened cabin. I was much too excited to sleep. I kept thinking about what kind of story idea I could come up with that might make a difference. Something that would help audiences understand what it was like to be Black and young and afraid of growing up in a world that saw us as a threat.

The sun was up when we landed early Sunday morning. The airport was quiet, almost deserted. It was freezing when we stepped out of the terminal. I only had on a thin jacket, which was fine for winter in L.A. but definitely unqualified for the East Coast. I stepped back inside while Dada called for a car service. When the SUV finally showed up, we were on our way home. Since I hadn't slept on the plane, my eyes felt a heaviness I couldn't fight, so I gave in and fell into a deep sleep.

Mom shook me awake when we arrived at our apartment building. Maybe it was because I had just awakened, but everything looked smaller. The apartment building, the steps leading up to the entrance, even the scrawny tree out front that was a pit stop for neighborhood dogs looked smaller. The cleaning-product smell in the elevator was stronger than I remembered. The screech as the elevator door opened on our floor seemed louder than before. Dada took out his keys to unlock our door, and it seemed strange. At Destiny's house, we punched a code on a keypad to unlock the doors. It had been so long since I'd even seen my house keys, I wondered where they were.

I told myself that I was feeling so strange because I was sleepy. I had at least eight hours of shut-eye to catch up on. So I went directly to my room, closed the door, and crawled under the covers.

A buzzing sensation on my thigh woke me. Were there bees in my bed? I reached down and realized it was my phone, still in my pocket. It was just before nine in the morning and there was a text message.

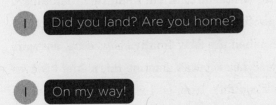

Honestly, I could have used a few more hours of sleep, but I was excited to see my bestie. I yawned, stretched, peeled my eyelids back, and looked around the room. For an instant, I wasn't sure whose room it was. I mean, I knew it was my room, but . . . I had the strange feeling that someone else lived there. Someone who used to be me but wasn't me anymore.

My Beyoncé and Queen posters were still on the wall, but I didn't have the same sense of awe that I used to when I looked up at them. After the experience of doing several photo shoots, I understood how much work went into them. Choosing the right clothes, getting your hair and makeup done, sitting around for hours while lights were set up, and then posing endlessly. It took a lot to get that perfect shot that would be used in magazines and posters.

I sat up in bed and looked across the room at my desk and my favorite swivel chair—they looked smaller than before. Even my twin bed felt super-tiny, and the walls of my room felt closer. Of course, our apartment was one hundred times smaller than where we'd been staying at Destiny Manaconda's, but I never expected to feel like an alien in my own room.

Things started to feel more normal when Dada came back from the supermarket with all the fixings needed to make French toast. I washed my face, brushed my teeth, and put on an old pair of pajamas. I was hanging out in the kitchen with Dada, completely forgetting Izzy was on her way until I heard knocking at the door.

Dada looked up from dipping bread in the egg and cinnamon mixture. "Who is that this early?"

Mom came out of her bedroom. "Who knows we're back already?"

"Izzy!" I said, as I ran across the room and flung the door open. To my complete surprise, Izzy was standing there with a broad smile, along with Hailey Joanna and just about all of the dramanerds from school!

They shouted, "Welcome home!" About twenty kids filed into our apartment. I was shocked, flabbergasted, gob-smacked, and then some. Here I was, in pajamas, my hair a mess of tangles, surrounded by kids looking at me with starry-eyed wonder.

Mom, hands on her hips, said, "What in the world is going on here?"

"Good morning, Mrs. Fuller." Hailey Joanne stepped forward. "Sorry to barge in like this, but we just couldn't wait to see our girl again."

Izzy added, "We wanted to be the first, so it'd be official."

"Official? What?"

"We are the first Mango Delight Fan Club!" All the kids piled around the living room cheering, "Mango! Mango! Mango!"

"All right, all right, calm down," Mom said. "It's too early for this kind of noise. Mango, why didn't you tell us about this?"

"I didn't know, Mom."

Hailey Joanne said, "She didn't. This was a surprise."

"It was all our idea, because we missed our girl so much," Izzy said. "We'll leave and come back later if you want."

I felt embarrassed for my friends. They meant well. I said, "Mom, do they have to go?"

Mom sighed and looked to Dada, who said, "I bought two loaves of bread and two dozen eggs, enough French toast for everybody."

As my friends cheered, my eyes glistened with appreciation for Dada. His spirit was so generous. Mom shook her head, smiling. She appreciated him, too. She held her hands up for quiet. "I guess you call can stay, but please keep the noise down; we don't want our neighbors complaining about us before we get settled back in."

Dada's chef experience came in handy as he and Mom prepared French toast for all of us. I barely had time to eat because the questions were coming so fast. "What's the show about?" "How does it feel to be a star?" "Do you like TV better than the stage?" "Do you get free clothes and everything?" "What's Destiny Manaconda's house like?" "Where's TJ?" And on and on. I was jet-lagged and, as happy as I was to see everyone, my energy supply kept getting smaller and my answers to their questions shorter.

After a couple of hours, Mom said, "It was nice of you all to drop by, but we've got unpacking to do, and Mango needs her rest." There were groans all around, but my friends hugged me on their way out and kept saying how good it was to have me back again.

Hailey Joanne and Izzy helped collect all the paper plates and cups from around the room and were the last to leave. At the door, Izzy joked, "I'll come by to pick you up for school tomorrow, in case you forgot the way."

"School?"

"Yeah. Aren't you coming back while you're here?"

"*Umm*. No, actually."

Hailey Joanne said, "Why not?"

"Well, my tutor from the studio prepared lessons for me. And I'm supposed to work with her on Face2Face until I go back to L.A."

"Really?" Izzy frowned. "We thought you'd want to be in school with us so we could hang like we used to."

"I do, but . . ."

"We understand," Hailey Joanne said, looking pointedly at Izzy. "She probably has a whole different curriculum from us. And you know, everybody would be staring at her all day, asking for autographs and stuff like that."

Izzy shrugged. "Well, all right. But can we stop by after?"

"Yeah! Come by and we'll hang."

Things felt a little strained as they left, and I wondered if I should have chosen to go back to Trueheart, so I could spend the three weeks with my friends. It was Jericka's suggestion that we tutor virtually with Aunt Joyce, because she wanted to make sure I got enough rest at home. She said, "I know you're excited to be going home and you'll want to hang out all day and night with your friends, but remember, it's only three weeks, and you still have a lot of work to do when you get back. Don't wear yourself out. Pace yourself, so you'll be one hundred percent when we resume production."

I promised her I'd take things easy, but from the look on Izzy's face as she was leaving, I wondered if that was a promise I should break.

CHAPTER THIRTY-FOUR

On the Run

Jet lag is no joke. By around four in the afternoon I got super-sleepy trying to watch a soccer match with Dada. I kept dozing off with my mouth hanging open and drool dripping down my chin. I was jarred awake when one of the teams scored, and Dada jumped up and shouted, "Goal! Goal! Goal!" I had had enough, although I usually enjoyed watching sports with him. I went to my room and lay on my bed. Just as I was getting comfortable, I got a text from TJ.

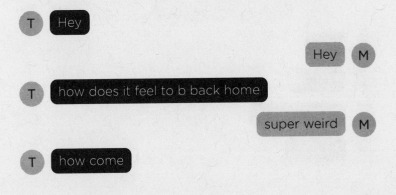

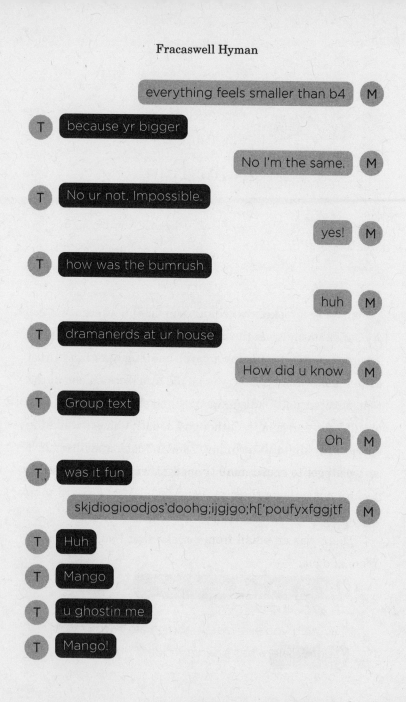

When I finally woke up at five-thirty in the morning, Dada was already up. I could hear him moving around in the kitchen. I picked up my phone and saw the end of my conversation with TJ. I laughed. "Lite weight." Yeah, I guess so.

It made me feel good that we were still friends, in spite of his relationship with Kashara. In fact, it made me feel good that we were all friends, especially since Kashara, Symphony, and I kind of got off to a rocky start. Working so closely together, we got to know each other pretty quickly. As work wound down during the last week, I wasn't as extra-busy as I normally was with recording, photo shoots, and interviews, so we all got to spend more time together. I was surprised to feel myself missing them already and looking forward to us all being back together.

There was an email from Jericka that had been sent to Mom and me:

> Mango and Margie
> So glad you all made it home safe and
> sound. There has been a request from your
> local afternoon TV news program *LIVE at 4*

to interview Mango on Monday's program.
It's a "hometown girl makes good" sort
of thing. We feel this would be excellent
publicity for the show. Hoping you agree
to do it. Just in case, Voza is sending an
outfit by overnight mail that will arrive by
noon. I'll arrange for hair and makeup and
send location and interview specifics in the
morning.

Best, Jericka

Well, there goes my "staycation." I hadn't been home a whole day, and there was work lined up. I was warned that there might be some local publicity to do while I was away, but I didn't think it would start so fast.

I spent some time in bed going over ideas I had for a *Mango All the Time* script. I had one idea where Mango went back in time as Harriet Tubman, helping enslaved people get to freedom. But what did that have to do with what happened to Dada and me? I wanted to write something that had to do with being stopped by the police just for being Black. I had learned in school that enslaved people always had to have written passes whenever they were off the plantation, because the paddy rollers—groups of armed White men patrolling for runaway slaves—would stop them to make sure they weren't runaways. Maybe I could do something with that . . . ?

No! I rejected that idea because I didn't want to play an enslaved person.

I was still figuring out different scenarios at six-thirty when Dada knocked at my door, "Mango-gal, you up for run?"

"Yeah! Be right there." Ever since our run up Sunset Plaza Drive, I'd gotten more and more into running again. It really did clear my mind and give me more energy for the day ahead. Dada and I walked to the park two blocks away. We warmed up and set off running through the cold, brisk air. This was the first time being back at home felt normal.

Mom was setting up Jasper's breakfast when we got back. "Mango, did you see the email from Jericka?"

"Yes."

"You okay with it?"

"Uh-huh."

"I just got off the phone with her. She's sending over a makeup lady," Mom checked the pad where she'd taken notes, "Carol Rasheed. She's bringing a stylist to do your hair. They'll be here at two o'clock, and we'll head over to the TV station at three. Okay?"

"Yes, that's good." I headed off to take a shower. My plan was to do my schoolwork and chill before the glam squad arrived, but then Dada reminded me: "What about your friends? Aren't they coming by after school?"

Uh-oh. I'd forgot about that. Judging by the disappointed look on Izzy's face as she was leaving the day before, I didn't think a phone call or a text would be good enough to change our plans. I decided I would hurry to do my schoolwork, head over to school, and meet them for lunch. I thought I could keep everyone happy that way. I should have thought again. . . .

CHAPTER THIRTY-FIVE

Mob Scene

Instead of just showing up empty-handed, I decided to bring lunch for my friends. I asked Dada to drive me to McDonald's and buy enough fries and chicken nuggets to feed around twenty dramanerds! Dada asked, "Are you sure you want to do this?"

"Yeah, this is a way to show everybody how much I miss them and care about them."

He was skeptical. "I know you're doing this out of the kindness of your heart, Mango-gal, but you don't want it to appear like you're showing off or buying friendships."

"These are all my friends, Dada. I don't have to buy their friendship. And I'm not showing off, I mean, come on, it's just McDonalds."

He drove me to McDonalds, where I got what was probably their largest lunch order of the day. When we were in L.A., Jericka and Mom set up a bank account for me with my own debit card so I wouldn't have to carry cash wherever

I went. The biggest chunk of money I was being paid went directly into a trust account that I couldn't access until I was twenty-one years old, but a percentage was added to my bank account regularly. It wasn't a lot, but it was way more than my usual allowance. I'd been so busy with work, I'd never gotten a chance to use my debit card. Paying for this lunch was the very first time, and it was kind of exciting.

The lunch bell was ringing as we pulled up in front of Trueheart Middle School. Dada asked, "You want me to lug the bags in for you?" There were two large plastic McDonald's shopping bags, but I could handle them, so I said no. Besides, I kind of wanted to make a grand entrance.

I was excited to be back at school, anticipating how my friends would be happy to see me and get a break from the regular lunch. It was awkward opening the door to the cafeteria while holding the two bags. I finally got it open, stepped in, and scanned the room looking for my friends.

Then it happened. I don't know if I was recognized first or if the two large bags from McDonald's drew the attention to me, but I quickly felt as though all eyes were on me with a laser focus.

I spotted Izzy and my dramanerd friends across the lunchroom at the usual tables. As I headed toward them, some kids got up from where they were seated and started following me. Someone yelled out, "Hey, it's Mango!" This caused an instant commotion. There was a loud rumble of shouts, chairs being pushed back, and footsteps tumbling toward me. Kids came at me from all directions. I was surrounded and couldn't make my way through the mob. I was pulled and pushed from all sides. Hands were reaching toward me. There were screams and shouts of excitement. I was pulled this way and that way. At one point I was moving across the room, but my feet weren't on the ground. I let go of the bags to cover my face with my hands, and kids made a dive for the food. Teachers yelled, "Back up! Everyone go to your seats now! Move away!"

I had my head down, trying to protect myself, when an adult made her way through the crowd and put her arms around me, shouting, "Everyone back off now!" The frenzy began to die down. As the kids backed away, I could see fries and chicken nuggets scattered all across the floor. I felt dizzy and disoriented, and I struggled to catch my breath. I knew the kids weren't trying to hurt me, but I was trembling anyway.

I kept my head down while the woman with her arms around me led me out of the cafeteria. When I finally looked at her, I couldn't believe my eyes. The stout penguin-shaped body. The bleached-blonde bouquet of curls. My rescuer was none other than Zippy Levy. The same Zippy who was in the cast of the Off-Off-Off-Broadway production of *Yo Romeo!* Zippy and I were not friends. We tolerated each other during the run of the show, but now she was a teacher at my old school and had rescued me. I was grateful and thought things might be different between us now, especially since Izzy and Hailey Joanne had only good things to say about her, but . . .

She led me into the teachers' lounge and shut the door. I sat on the sofa, trying to stop my hands from trembling. Zippy stood over me, smirking and shaking her head. "Well, well, well, look who's here. Causing a commotion. What the heck were you thinking?"

"Huh? I was coming for lunch. . . ."

"You're not enrolled here. You don't have any business being here."

"I know, but—"

"You almost caused a riot, Mango."

"I'm sorry, I didn't expect—I just wanted to see my friends and bring them some lunch."

Zippy let out a dismissive cackle, "Oh, so the big, rich TV star decides to show up with lunch for the peasants! I get it. You want to show off how much money you're making, right? I bet you tried to start a riot on purpose."

"I did not! I just wanted to see my friends!"

"You could have seen them after school."

"I can't! I have an TV interview on *Live at 4* after school."

"Is that so? . . ." Zippy's eyes narrowed as she glowered at me. "Let me tell you something, Mango Delight—you're not special. You just got lucky. It's like getting hit by a bolt of lightning. It happens to one in a million, and I guess you're that one. Great. *Fan-freaking-tastic*! But believe you me, there are plenty of people way more talented than you right here in this school, so don't come in here acting all high and mighty, looking down your nose at the rest of us."

I stood up, "I'm not looking down my nose at anyone, I just came to see my friends!"

Zippy moved in so close we were almost nose to nose. I could smell her split pea soup breath as she said, "You don't have any friends here, kiddo. You've got fans. And there's a BIG difference!"

Was what she said true? It completely caught me off guard. All of these feelings were welling up inside me. I was a volcano about to erupt hot tears. I knew Zippy resented me and had it in for me back in New York. I knew she was jealous, because I had gone so far so fast in my career, but did she have to be so mean? Were other people thinking and feeling the way she felt toward me? Did I really have fans instead of friends?

I didn't want to let Zippy see my cry. That'd be a triumph for her. I pushed past her and ran out of the teachers' lounge. I headed straight for the exit. I heard some call, "Mango wait!" It might have been Izzy, but I didn't stop to look. I just ran and ran and ran until I got home, where I shut myself in my room and practically cried my eyes out.

When the hair and makeup team arrived, my eyes were red, my face swollen, and my feelings fragile. Mom kept asking what was wrong, and Dada wanted to know if anything bad happened at school, but I didn't want to talk about it. It would only make matters worse if Mom found out how Zippy had bullied me. She still hadn't forgiven Zippy for letting me get lost on the subway when I was in New York.

There were a stream of text messages from Izzy and Hailey Joanne, but I didn't read them. I knew they'd want to talk about what happened, and I didn't. The whole situation felt like a big, ugly bruise that was too painful to touch.

The hair and makeup team was very nice and professional. Carol Rasheed and the hairdresser started off making general small talk, but they realized I wasn't in the mood and went about their jobs quietly. I hope they didn't think I was snobby or stuck up. But to be honest, in the moment I didn't care what they thought. My feelings were too raw to act any other way. It took all the strength I had just to hold it together so I'd be prepared for the interview.

When it was time to get dressed, I hadn't even opened the garment bag with the clothes Voza sent from L.A. There was a lavender cashmere ankle-length cardigan; a cashmere turtleneck; high-waist, deep-purple sequined pants; and yellow leather ankle-length boots. I thought it was a bit dressy for an afternoon interview, but that was Voza, always ahead of the trends. Normally, I would've spent a lot of time in the mirror admiring the clothes and snapping selfies, but I wasn't in the mood. Mom took some pictures of me and sent them to Voza and Jericka for their approval. I couldn't bring myself to smile, no matter how much Mom coached me to "brighten up!"

Jericka texted immediately:

J

You look great! Why so sad?

thanks. Long day. M

J understood. Remember your talking points for the interview. Show premiere date. Album release date. Positivity plus a sprinkling of the personal makes for great interviews!

I sent her a 👍 and closed my phone. Mom called a car service, and we headed for the studio. Dada, who was staying home with Jasper, said, "Be brilliant! We'll be watching, Mango-gal."

At the studio, we waited in the green room until it was time for my interview. Mom was on her iPad answering a stream of emails from Jericka and the studio. She was enjoying her job as Jericka's assistant and becoming a wiz at updating the website the publicity department had set up for me.

When it was time for the interview, I was taken to the set by a production assistant. Joy James, the host of *Live at 4* gave me a warm smile and introduced herself. We took our places on the set. As the stage manager gave the countdown, "In five, four, three, . . ." I armed myself with all my media training and put on a bright smile. Was I being phony and fake or professional and prepared? I couldn't tell, but this was a job, and I was determined to do it well.

I wasn't the rookie who had stared at her image on the monitor like a deer in headlights the way I had on my first television interview months ago. No, now I knew how to act like I was excited to be there and pretend it was the first time I was asked the same questions I'd been asked a hundred times before.

The interview was going well until Joy surprised me with a curveball. "I heard you caused quite as stir when you showed up at your school today. Can you tell me what happened?"

How had she found out about that? Who would have told her? No one at school knew about my interview except . . . Zippy. Of course. The evil minion probably called *Live at 4* and told them what had happened, just to be mean. I took me about three seconds to put all of this together, but I refused to be stumped by the ambush question. I smiled brightly and said, "Oh yes, that was so much fun. I stopped by for lunch with my friends, and things got a little bit out of hand with all the excitement, but it was all love. So great to be back!" I could tell Joy wanted a more scoop-worthy answer, but I maintained my poise and gave her a "next question" smile, and we carried on.

On the way home, Mom asked me about lunch at school. "Did something bad happen? Is that why you've been so glum all afternoon?"

I gave her the same sunny smile and performance I had given on TV. "It was nothing, Mom. Just excitement and fun." Phony or professional? I wasn't quite sure anymore.

CHAPTER THIRTY-SIX
A Hitch in the Plan

B ack at home, Dada told me that Hailey Joanne and Izzy
dropped by after school. "They seemed a bit worried about
you. I told them to come back later and join us for dinner. Is
that okay with you?" I nodded, yes. As I was heading for my
room, he stopped me. "You got a call from the principal of
your school."

"Miss Lipschultz?"

"Yes." He handed me a slip of paper. "She left a number
for you to call her back. She said it was urgent."

As I took the paper, I thought to myself, *Uh-oh. Just
what I need, to be chewed out over what happened at lunch
by the woman with the coldest gray eyes south of the North
Pole.* I went to my room and sat on the bed with my phone
in my hands. *Should I call her back now? Did I have the
energy after what I'd already gone through today? If I didn't
call her back, would she call again? Would she talk to Mom
about what had happened? That would just lead to more*

trouble for me. So, I put on my imaginary *big girl pants* and dialed.

The phone rang a few times. I was expecting the school secretary to pick up, but Ms. Lipschultz answered. She said, "I'm driving, and you're on speakerphone; can you hear me okay?"

"Yes."

"Great. We're so happy to have you back in town, Mango, even if it's just for a short visit."

"Thank you." I was surprised that she was being so nice. Had the Ice Queen melted?

"I was informed about what happened at lunch today. I'm so sorry. I blame myself. The excitement about one of our own becoming a television star has been building since the beginning of the school year. Of course, the students would be ecstatic to see a real TV star in their midst. I was planning on getting in touch with you and arranging a special assembly where you could tell us all about your experiences and take questions from the students. Would you be willing to do that if I set it up?"

For a moment, I couldn't speak. I had been so sure she was going to lecture me about just showing up at school even though I wasn't enrolled there anymore. Instead she was pitching an event. All I could get out of my mouth was, "*Ummmmm . . .*"

"I know, I'm just springing this on you, so why don't you take your time and think about it. Give me a call tomorrow and let me know your decision. It's okay if you're too busy or don't feel like it. I'll understand. But there really is a lot of love for you at Trueheart, and I want us all to have a chance to show you just how much in a proper way. Okay? Talk soon!"

She clicked off. I lay back on the bed, staring up at the ceiling. How strange it was that a few hours ago I was told I didn't belong there, and I wasn't special. Now the opposite. Was my life always going to be like a seesaw? Up one minute, down the next?

I had changed into my jeans and T-shirt and put away the clothes Voza sent me, so Mom could mail them back to L.A. I was all set when Izzy and Hailey Joanne arrived. I hurried them into my room. I didn't want to talk about the mob scene at lunch in front of my parents. If they found out, they'd never let me leave the house or go anywhere on my own ever again. Izzy and Hailey Joanne sat on the bed. I sat on my swivel desk chair.

"We saw your interview on TV. Why didn't you tell us yesterday?" Izzy asked.

"I didn't know about it until this morning. That's why I came for lunch. I wanted to fill you in and make up for not being able to meet you after school."

"Oh, Mango," Hailey Joanne said, "You don't have anything to make up for. We know you're busy. You could have texted us. We would've understood."

That was a relief. "Thanks. I just didn't want you to think I was taking you for granted or acting like a big star or anything."

"News flash!" Izzy stood and struck a very dramatic pose, "You ARE a big star! At least you are to all of us. But the two of us right here, right now, we're your *friend-friends*. We care about you, boo!"

I started feeling all warm inside. I thought back to what Zippy had said about having fans instead of friends. She was wrong when it came to these two.

"It was really smooth the way you described what happened at school." Hailey Joanne said.

"My media training kicked in, and I didn't want to say anything negative."

"That's good, because nobody meant to harm you; we were just excited, that's all."

"Yeah, excited and hungry," Izzy said. "What happened to those fries and chicken nuggets was an epic tragedy! Especially since it was split pea soup day and that's the one lunch I can do without."

Mom came my door. "Mango, I just got off the phone with Jericka. Something's come up, and . . . well, she needs to talk to you."

"Now?"

"It's kind of a big deal. I think you should give her a call." Mom looked at the girls. "You all want to come into the living room while Mango talks to her manager?"

"No, Mom, it's okay. They can stay. I want Jericka to meet them."

"Okay. If you're sure." Mom left, closing the door behind her.

I punched in the speed-dial code for Jericka and waited. Izzy said, "*OMGZ*, we are actually going to be in the room when you talk to your real Hollywood manager!"

"Get a grip, Isabel." Hailey Joanne rolled her eyes. "Maybe we should leave the room if you're going to be obnoxious."

"Obnoxious? You've got a lot of nerve and SAT words! If I go, you go."

"No. Stay. Both of you." I wanted to share what my life was like with the girls I was closest to. They had been so understanding about today. I knew I could trust them.

Jericka answered the phone, "Hi, Mango."

"Hi, I'm here with my two best friends, Izzy and Hailey Joanne. Do you mind if I put you on speaker?" Izzy silently clapped her hands and jiggled up and down on the bed, and Hailey Joanne side-eyed her.

"I don't mind if you don't. But this is a business call."

"That's okay." I put her on speaker.

"There's good news and not-so-good-news. Which do you want first?"

Izzy said, "Always take the good new first, girl. It's easier to come down when you're up than to go up when you're down."

I guess that made sense, so I said, "Give me the good news."

"We've finally found the perfect theme song for the show, and it was written by your guys, Bob and Larry."

"Really!"

Izzy threw herself back across the bed and wriggled in spasms. "*OMGZ!* I can't take it! I just can't TAKE IT!"

"Isabel!" Hailey Joanne glared, "Stop before you break the bed!"

Trying to not laugh at Izzy's antics, I asked, "What's the song called? When do I get to hear it?"

"It's called *Mango All the Time,* and trust me, it's great. I heard it a couple of times and can't get it out of my head. It's not only going to be the show's theme song, but E.B. wants it to be your first single. I'm going to send you a link to hear the demo in the morning. Bob and Larry are making a few tiny adjustments and rerecording it as we speak."

I still wasn't thrilled about my name being in the title of the show and now the theme song, but I was happy that Bob and Larry were the composers. Some of the songs I had already recorded for the show were good but not exactly top-of-the-chart hits. At least, that's the way I felt. TJ thought they were bubblegum, but our live audiences had liked them, so maybe Dionne and the producers knew what they were doing.

Izzy finally calmed down and said, "Okay, what about the bad news."

Jericka chuckled. "Well, it's not that bad, but unfortunately we're going to have to bring you back to L.A. two weeks earlier than planned, Mango."

My thrill spilled. "What? No! Why?"

"We need to get you in the studio and get the song recorded and mixed, so we can release it to radio and streaming services ahead of the premiere. E.B. also wants us to produce a music video right away."

"Oh, man, talk about bad news!" Izzy flung herself back on the bed again.

Hailey Joanne stomped her feet, "No way! We were planning a big party and everything!"

"It's not fair, Jericka. Why can't I record the song here?"

"Bob and Larry are out here in L.A., and the concept of the video takes place on the set. Besides, that's the way E.B. wants it."

"Who is this E.B. anyway?" Hailey Joanne demanded.

"Eyebrows. He's the head of the studio. Whatever he says goes."

"Listen, girls," Jericka said, "It's not all bad. E.B. is really committed to this project. He's arranged to have a big Hollywood premiere, like they do for movies. That's another reason you'll need to come back early, Mango. Voza needs you for fittings, and there will be more interviews once the song and video are released."

From the looks of my two friends on the bed, maybe I shouldn't have kept them in the room for this phone call. I was used to all the extra work I had to do. I mean, yeah, my name was in the title of the show. I had learned that the extra load came with the territory. I was quiet for a while, and Jericka said, "Mango? Are you still there?"

"Yeah, I'm just . . . I don't know, I wanted to be with my friends for the premiere."

"Well . . ." Jericka paused for a moment. "Perhaps if you can't be with your friends, maybe I can arrange for your friends to be with you."

Izzy and Hailey Joanne perked up.

"What? What do you mean?"

"We can fly them out for the premiere as your guests. If we can clear it with their parents."

All three of us *SCREAMED* so loud and for so long, Mom came rushing into the room. "What's going on?"

Izzy, tears streaming down her face, grabbed my mom in a bear hug and shouted, "We're going to Hollywood, that's what's going on!"

CHAPTER THIRTY-SEVEN

The Thing About Snow . . .

The next morning, I called Principal Lipschultz and agreed to do the special assembly at the end of the week. We discussed TJ appearing virtually on the big screen in the auditorium. Voza called and offered to send me a special outfit for the event, but I said I just wanted to be my T-shirt and jeans self and feel comfortable sharing my experiences with my friends and my fans. I didn't want to disappoint Jericka, Eyebrows, or the studios, but I politely turned down any more interviews while I was at home. I was really glad that Mom and Dada backed me up on this. Since my time was shortened, I wanted to spend as much time being regular Mango as possible.

Jericka sent me a link to the new theme song for the show. I was nervous about listening to it, so I hesitated. *What if I didn't like it? Would they change it, or would I have to sing it anyway? And if I didn't like it and I said so, would that make Bob and Larry feel some kind of way?* I kept imagining all sorts of gloomy scenarios about my reaction to the song when I finally made myself snap out of it. What if I *did* like the song? I wouldn't know until I listened to it. I didn't understand why I jumped to the negative so quickly. Tons of great things were happening to me and for me. I needed to learn how to trust myself and be confident. So, I went to my room, put in my earbuds, and pressed the link.

Thankfully, the song was great! The lyrics were clever in the way they used the word "time." Mango was *right on time, ahead of her time, never wasting time, traveling through time, managing her time, bending her time, spending her time being Mango All the Time.* I thought it was cute, and I couldn't wait to sing it! I sent a group text to Jericka, Dionne, Bob, and Larry telling them how much I loved the song, and it was worth coming back early to record it and make a music video. *Phew*! All that worry, and all I had to do was listen.

I met up with Izzy and Hailey Joanne after school. I was partially hidden while waiting for them across the street near Sal's Pizzeria. I was wearing a baseball cap, dark sunglasses, and the hood of my coat up over my head. It was fun trying to be incognito, like I was a big star even though I wasn't. The show hadn't even premiered on television yet, but the kids at my school knew all about me, and I didn't want to be recognized or cause another incident.

We had planned to go to Crystal Plaza, a posh indoor mall near Hailey Joanne's neighborhood, because it was too cold to go to the old outdoor mall, which was closer to where

Izzy and I lived. Then we were going to have a sleepover at Hailey Joanne's, but I could tell from the looks on their faces as they walked up to me that something was wrong. Hailey Joanne said, "Sorry Mango, I have to cancel our plans and go to a Jack and Jill meeting."

"What's that?"

"It's a club for rich Black kids." Izzy said, frowning.

"It is not only for rich Black kids, Isabel. It's an organization for African American mothers and daughters to help girls develop into future leaders."

"Oh . . . How come I never heard of it before?"

"Because," Izzy said, "you're not rich enough . . . at least not yet."

Hailey Joanne rolled her eyes, her lips pressed together in a tight line, and she spoke through gritted teeth. "Isabel, I know you're just trying to get on my nerves because you're disappointed that we have to cancel our plans, so I'm gonna give you a pass on your snide remarks."

"Oh, thanks so much, Your Royal Highness."

"Izzy, come on now; it's not her fault."

"Thank you, Mango. It's not like I don't want to hang out with you all, but Mother is a leader in the organization, and I *have* to be there." Hailey Joanne hugged me before she left. She tried to hug Izzy, but I could tell it was like putting her arms around an ironing board.

I called Mom and told her the sleepover plans had been canceled, and I would be home for dinner. Izzy and I decided we'd go window-shopping at the old outdoor mall, even though it was so cold, we could see our breath when we exhaled. Izzy was silent on the way, which was really strange if you knew her. So, I said, "Why so quiet?"

"It's just that we don't have a lot of time to spend together before you leave, and she has to run off to her snooty meeting."

"It's not her fault, and you know that."

"Whatever . . ."

From the way Izzy was brooding, I knew something else was bothering her,

So I asked, "What's really bugging you?"

Izzy stopped and turned to me. "I don't know. It's a mixture of things."

"Like what?"

"Like I'm losing my best friend before we even had time to hang out, and . . ." Izzy was about to say something. I could tell it was on the tip of her tongue, but instead of spitting it out, she shook her head, turned, and started walking again. I followed her.

"And what?"

"I don't want to be, I really don't, but—I'm jealous of you."

"Izzy, I'm sorry."

"You don't have anything to be sorry about. You didn't zoom ahead of me and become a big star on purpose. It just happened. What makes me jealous is that it happened to you and not to me."

I didn't know what to say. It was obvious Izzy was hurting, and that's why I wanted to say I was sorry. I didn't want her to be hurt, but what could I do about it?

"You know, Mango, I spend so much time wishing I were you. Wishing I could trade places with you. The more I wish I were you, the more I'm not satisfied being me. Then I start picking myself apart. Maybe if I were thinner. Maybe if I were taller? Maybe if I were a better singer."

"You're a great singer, and you're beautiful!"

"I know, I know. But still . . . everything I ever wanted just fell into your lap, and—I can't help it, I get jealous. I try to hide it, but it just pops out, like . . . I guess I'm angry about Hailey Joanne not coming with us because when it's the three of us, I have someone regular, more like me. I mean, I'm not all *la-dee-dah* rich like she is, but when she's around, I don't feel like I'm alone in your shadow."

I never meant to make Izzy feel the way she felt. That was out of my control. It was scary to think that the more famous you became, the more people had ideas and opinions about you that had nothing to do with who you really were. Even people who knew you, thought about you differently and sometimes compared themselves to you in ways that made them feel bad. I didn't want to affect anyone that way, especially not my friends.

All I wanted more than anything was to come back home and feel normal for a while, and here I was, standing on the street, watching my friend feel bad about herself because she was comparing her life to mine. I stopped walking. Izzy stopped and turned toward me. I gave her a big hug and whispered, "We both know you're super-talented, beautiful, and amazing, Isabel Otero. One day the whole world is going to know it, too. No doubt."

As we hugged, a snowflake landed on the tip of my nose. I looked up, and tiny lace tufts of white were falling from the sky. Izzy looked up, too, and said, "*OMGZ*, Mango, do you know what this is?"

"Yeah, it's snow."

"I know, but do you know what it means?"

"Uh . . . it's winter?"

"Mango! You just told me the whole world was going to know I'm super-talented, beautiful, and amazing, and then it started to snow! It's a sign! Like a prophecy or something! What you said is absolutely going to come true!"

Izzy threw her head back, and with arms open wide, she began to spin around and around, faster and faster, laughing. I couldn't help myself. I threw my head back, opened my arms. and began to spin around fast, too. People passing by must've thought we were crazy, but I didn't care. At that moment, all I cared about was hoping I was right and Izzy's wishes would come true.

CHAPTER THIRTY-EIGHT

SWB

After spinning until we were so dizzy that we banged into each other, Izzy and I sang Beyoncé songs on our way to the mall. Izzy wanted to go to Charisma Cosmetics, a store that specialized in makeup and perfume. I wasn't as excited about going there as she was. I spent most of my days having makeup applied for the show or for interviews or photo sessions. Then at home, Mom had me on a strict skin-care regimen to avoid breakouts and other damage from so many cosmetics. Still, my bestie didn't have the same experience with foundation, eye shadow, eyeliner, eyelashes, and contour brushes, so I pretended to be happy to go to Charisma Cosmetics, too. *Phony or friendly?* Again, I wasn't sure.

We flitted around the store from counter to counter, trying whatever samples were available. From the moment we entered, I had the feeling that we were being subtly watched, but I didn't want to let that bother me. We weren't doing anything wrong and had no intention of shoplifting, so I didn't care.

At a display of makeup brushes, I was explaining the different uses of each brush. "This one is for contouring and this one is for blending." When I picked up a large set of brushes in a fancy lacquer and rhinestone-encrusted case, a saleswoman rushed over and snatched it out of my hands. Stunned at the rudeness, I said, "Excuse me?"

She looked down her nose at me. "These are very expensive brushes. They're mink, from France, actually. They are well out of your price range."

Izzy said, "How would you know what's in or out of her price range?"

"Let me be frank, I'm running out of patience. It's clear that you have no intention of purchasing anything, and you've been walking around touching the merchandise for twenty-five minutes. I believe it's time for you to leave the store."

Izzy looked at the saleswoman curiously. "How do you know how long we've been in here?"

"Because, Izzy, she's been spying on us since we walked in the door."

The saleswoman pointed her finger in my face, "I'm not spying, I'm simply protecting our merchandise. And there are certain things that are just beyond your means."

I felt so irritated, I reached into my pocket and pulled out my ATM card. I wanted to show this pinch-faced person pointing her finger in my face that her assumptions about the kind of person I was and what I could afford were wrong. "How much are the mink brushes?"

"Two hundred dollars for the set."

"Is that all? I'll take them. In fact, I'll take a set for me and a set for my friend."

"Mango!" Izzy protested, "I don't want those."

"Neither do I."

"So why're you buying them?"

"I want to show her that she can't tell who I am or what I can afford by the color of my skin!"

The saleswoman's face reddened. "I didn't say anything about the color of your skin."

"You didn't say anything, but your actions did. You started following us the second we walked through the door." Some of the other customers, who were mostly White, were listening. I pointed to them. "Why didn't you follow any of them?" The saleswoman didn't respond. She just smirked at me. I held out my ATM card out to her.

"Mango, no! Don't spend four hundred dollars plus tax on stuff we both don't want just to prove a point. She's not worth it."

Izzy was right. Why should I make her sales book look good when what she did made me feel bad? My parents used to warn me whenever we went shopping, "*Keep your hands out of your pockets. Don't carry merchandise around the store. If you intend on buying something, take it straight to the register.*" They had prepared me early on for the perils of

SWB, *Shopping While Black*. Unfortunately, I had to become used to being looked at as suspicious simply because I was a Black girl. It wasn't fair that we couldn't just walk into a store without having to remind ourselves to be careful of how we appeared to others. I looked around at the shoppers watching. Most of them looked on sympathetically. Still, they couldn't walk in my shoes to see what it really felt like to always have to be on guard. I put my ATM card back in my pocket and said, "Come on, Izzy, let's get out of here."

As we headed for the exit, Izzy turned back to the saleswoman. "Just so you know, this girl here is Mango Delight. In a month, your kids will be watching her star in her own TV show and wishing they knew her. And guess what? I bet you won't tell the truth about how you met her and how badly you treated her, because you will be—and should be—ashamed."

Back out in the cold, Izzy seemed energized by what had just happened. I, on the other hand, felt drained and wanted to go home. On the way, I told Izzy that I was trying to figure out a way of addressing this kind of bias on the show, but I didn't know how. Izzy said, "Maybe something like what just happened to us can happen to your character on the show." That might work, but then what? I had been struggling to come up with an idea for weeks, and nothing seemed right. I got a chill that wasn't connected to the cold weather as I thought to myself, *Maybe I'm not a writer. Maybe I should just give up.*

. . .

When I got home, Mom informed me that we were going to have a family meeting. Family meetings usually happened when something big had occurred or something was about to change or I had done something that was temporarily unforgivable. I hadn't broken any rules or laws that I knew of, so I didn't let the upcoming meeting stress me out.

We waited until after dinner, because Jasper was too young to participate, even though what we were going to discuss would change his life. Mom had some website work to catch up on, so while Dada took care of the dishes, I bathed my little brother, read him a story, and put him to bed.

We gathered in the living room, Mom and Dada on the couch, and me crisscross applesauce on the floor in front of them. Mom cleared her throat. "Mango, honey, Dada and I have been discussing our living arrangements for the foreseeable future. We want to know how you feel about being back here at home?"

I shrugged. "I guess I feel okay. I mean, it's kind of weird, too. Everything seems smaller and different."

Dada slapped his hands on his knees. "Didn't I say the same thing, Margie? Especially the kitchen! It feels like I'm cooking in a closet now."

"That's because we've been spending so much time in a mansion," Mom said. "But that's temporary. If we did move to Los Angeles permanently, we wouldn't be living in a place that big and grand."

"Permanently?" I was beginning to realize what this family meeting was all about. "Who said we were moving there permanently?"

"We haven't made a final decision yet, but we have to be smart about what the next year or two could look like. And let's be real, it wouldn't make sense to keep paying rent on this apartment when we'd be living across the country most of the time."

Dada added, "If I take the executive chef job at Chaos we'd be living in Los Angeles year-round."

"Are you sure you want to take it?"

"Well, Mango-gal, it's a great opportunity. A dream, really. It would pay extremely well. And who knows? It could lead to me opening my own place."

"We know it might be hard for you to leave your friends and the things you know and are used to, but your career is on the rise and . . . well, what do you think?"

I looked around the living room, into the kitchen, down the short hall that led to the two bedrooms and bathroom. I thought about all the things that had happened in this apartment since we'd been here. I realized we'd only lived here a little more than a year. Dada moved us to this neighborhood to be closer to his job working at my ex-bestie Brooklyn's father's Italian restaurant. A little more than year ago, I started a new school, made and lost new friends, and had opportunities that changed my life in ways I never expected.

In that sense, this apartment had been a magical place. But it wasn't a forever home. It was a launching pad for the journey ahead. I liked California, the weather, the sun, and the vibe, as Chef Felipé would say. I knew Dada really liked it, too. I smiled and said, "Let's get to packing!"

CHAPTER THIRTY-NINE
"Just to Say Thank You"

You never know how much stuff you have collected until you start the process of moving. On Thursday after school, Izzy and Hailey Joanne came over to help me pack up my room. A lot of my clothes had already been sent to L.A., but there were sweaters, coats, boots, and tons of stuff that I wouldn't be caught dead in now that I was a teenager. Most of those clothes were in good shape, so I decided to donate them to Good Hope, an organization that sold gently used clothing at very reasonable prices.

Izzy said, "Some lucky girl is going to be wearing sweaters and pants that were worn by a star."

"But she'll never know," I said.

"Maybe you should write your name on the labels or something. That way, the kid who gets it can auction it off on eBay!"

Hailey Joanne looked from Izzy to me, raised an eyebrow, and shook her head. I giggled. Izzy was always coming up with starry-eyed fantasies. We were making good progress packing until I came across a box that held a lot of old pictures that never made it to photo albums. There were pictures of Izzy and me from when we first met in kindergarten. We all piled on the bed and cooed and laughed at how little we were and told stories recalling what a ham Izzy was, even back then. The poses that girl struck at five years old were hilarious.

Izzy said, "Wait until you see the poses I strike on the red carpet when we come out to Hollywood for your premiere."

"Oh, Isabel, please don't embarrass us," Hailey Joanne said.

"Embarrass? What could possibly be embarrassing about this—" Izzy got up from the bed and started strutting and posing around the room. "I can hear the paparazzi now, 'look over here, girls' and 'strike that pose again!'" We were laughing so hard at her clowning that Hailey Joanne and I jumped up from the bed and the three of us stood in front of the mirror doing our best super-model, red carpet poses, complete with duck lip pouts and glamazon glory!

Mom called from the living room, "Don't sound like there's much packing going on in there, ladies!"

We snapped out of our fantasy and got back to packing boxes. Izzy said, "The first thing I'm going to do when I get back from the premiere is take one of our red carpet photos to Charisma Cosmetics and show that bigoted saleswoman who she was dealing with."

As I was carefully taking down one of my Beyoncé posters, I asked, "Do you think that'll make her change?"

Izzy said, "I doubt it, but that doesn't mean we shouldn't try to open her eyes."

"Izzy's right. You can't just brush these things off like they were nothing. You have to speak up and speak out. My great-grandmother had to put up with a ton of prejudice when she started her business."

Our school, Irma Beth Trueheart Middle School, was named for Hailey Joanne's great-grandmother who became a millionaire at twenty-five years old. She was a hairdresser who invented a line of hair care products specifically for the texture of Black women's hair. When she became successful, she led the charge of integrating schools in our state. Irma Beth Trueheart was a real "S-hero."

"Do you know her homes, where she had salons, were burned to the ground five times? And it was impossible for her to get insurance because she was Black, and the banks considered her too big a risk. But my great-grandmother never gave up. She started selling her products door-to-door at first. Then she bought a little truck and kept it moving. When she became successful, she used a good deal of her money to start a company that insured Black business owners."

As Hailey Joanne told us more of her great-grandmother's struggle to overcome prejudice, we were mesmerized, stopped packing again, and sank down on the floor to listen. "She had crosses burned on her lawn, and one of her sons, Zaydock, was almost lynched. Luckily, Great-grandmother Irma Beth was able to get him out of town and on a train north before he was caught. If he had been caught, I wouldn't be here. He was my grandfather."

My parents didn't want me to go to a public school. They could afford to send me to any private school I'd want to attend, but I put my foot down and said no. I don't talk about this a lot, but every time I walk into our school I feel so proud of my great-grandmother. I wish I could travel back in time just for a moment, just enough time to hug her and tell her how grateful I am that she kept on fighting and never gave up, because she's responsible for the life I'm living today."

My brain exploded with ideas like fireworks! I leapt up from the floor, "That's it!"

"That's what?"

"The idea I need to for an episode of *Mango All the Time*!" I turned to Izzy. "Remember when you said I should use what happened to us in the store?" Izzy nodded. "Well, I can do that, and then Mango can go back in time to meet Irma Beth Trueheart!"

"For what?"

"Just to say thank you. To show gratitude for all the women and men and girls and boys who stood up against bigotry and prejudice. And to encourage the kids watching to keep standing up, no matter what."

I looked at Hailey Joanne to see what she thought, and her eyes were wet.

"Mango, that would mean so much to my family and me."
She hugged me, and I started crying. Izzy got up and made it
a group hug, and she started sniffling, too.

Mom came to the door and stood there with her hands on
her hips, staring at us. "What in the world? One minute y'all
are laughing like you lost your minds, and the next you're
boo-hooing like professional mourners. Can you please find a
way to keep your emotions in check and pack up this room?"

Wiping our eyes and blowing our noses, we got back to
packing. As we worked, we continued generating ideas about
how to make the story work. I became so excited, I couldn't
hold back a minute longer. I made a Face2Face call to Dionne
Harmony, and luckily she was available. I introduced my
friends, and together the three of us pitched the idea for the
episode from beginning to end. Dionne listened quietly, asked
a few questions here and there, then she said, "That sounds
like a winner. Wow, Mango, you did it."

"I didn't do it by myself. All three of us came up with ideas."

"Then I guess all three of you should write the script."

Our screams were epic. We were jumping and stamping on
the floor so hard, I imagine the people living in the apartment
below us thought there was a stampede over their heads.

From the kitchen, Mom called, "Mango? What in the
world is going on in there?"

We froze in place, holding our hands over our mouths.
Once we calmed down, Dionne said, "I'll need you girls to
write out a beat sheet."

Izzy said, "What's that?"

"Just sketch out what happens in the story step-by-step, just the way you pitched it to me. I'll go over it, give you some notes, and then you'll do a full scene-by-scene outline. Once that's approved, you write the script."

"Together?" Hailey Joanne asked.

"Yes."

"How? Mango will be in California, and we'll be here."

I said, "We can do it on Face2Face, just like we're doing now! And send stuff back and forth to each other and keep working on it until it's perfect."

Dionne said, "Sounds like a plan."

Izzy raised her hand. "*Ummm*. One question . . . will we be getting paid?"

"Of course. You'll be paid the union rate for a writing team."

Izzy stood up and started chanting and dancing around the room. "We gettin' paid! Oh yeah! We makin' bank! That's right!"

Hailey Joanne and I joined in high-stepping around the room. "We gettin' paid! Oh yeah! We makin' bank! That's right! We gettin' paid! Oh yeah! We makin' bank! That's right!" Even Dionne joined in on Face2Face. "We gettin' paid! Oh yeah! We makin' bank! That's right!"

Mom came to the door and with a look of utter exasperation said, "I glad y'all are gettin' paid, but I'm sure it ain't for packing up this room!"

CHAPTER FORTY

End of the Beginning

The assembly at Trueheart was on Friday at two in the afternoon, so that TJ, who was three hours behind us on the West Coast, wouldn't have to get up so early. Dionne had arranged to send some clips from the show to give the students an idea of what it would be like. Jericka got permission from Ms. Lipschultz for local news crews to be allowed to shoot some footage of the Q & A to use on their broadcasts. Somehow Mom and Dada got wind of what had happened in the lunchroom, so they insisted on Dada escorting me to school and requested that I be let in the building through the loading dock to avoid a repeat of lunchroom-gate.

Ms. Lipschultz was waiting outside to greet us when we arrived. She had a school security guard with her, which made me feel like a VIP and was also a little creepy at the same time—something about the uniform. . . .

Ms. Lipschultz said, "Let's go to my office. Can I get you anything to drink? Water? A coffee?"

I immediately said, "Coffee! Yes, please!"

Dada gave me "the look." "*Mangoooo*."

I sighed, foiled again in my quest for a cup of joe. "I'll have a bottled water."

"Nothing for me, thanks." Dada said.

"Would you like some fruit, trail mix, or chips?"

I said, "No, thank you," but then I wondered if there were some Hot Cheetos in the mix. I'd never say no to them.

We took seats in Ms. Lipschultz's office, and I couldn't help but remember the last time Dada and I were in there together. It was in the midst of all the drama when I was accused of drowning Brooklyn's phone. Back then I felt like a criminal being interrogated under blinding hot lights. I smiled and shook my head at the memory. I had never been so miserable as I was that day, and now things had changed so much. I was back in the same room, in the same seat, but this time I was a special guest being offered snacks and beverages by the principal whose mere gaze used to make my blood run cold. I thought to myself, *No matter how bad things get, if you just hold on, they'll get better.*

Ms. Lipschultz sat at her desk and got down to business. "First of all, thank you so much for doing this, Mango. It's an incredible gift to the school and all the students. We received a zip drive with scenes from the show, and the kids are all so excited to see what you've been doing." She was being so warm and friendly, even her gray eyes had lost their frosty glare. "We're going to begin by showing the clips from the

271

show. Then our moderator will introduce you, and after you are seated, she will introduce TJ, who will be joining us on Face2Face projected on the screen. When that's all settled, she'll start things off by asking each of you questions about your work. Then she'll open up the Q & A to the students and faculty. Any questions?"

"Yes, who's the moderator?"

"Oh, that's right, I neglected to tell you that Ms. Levy will moderate. Zippy is our new drama teacher, and she knows you so well, since you all worked together last summer—"

I interrupted. "No. I don't want Zippy to moderate."

Ms. Lipschultz seemed taken aback. "Oh. I thought you were friends. I mean, she intimated that—"

"We're not friends. Not even close."

"Mango-gal, don't be rude."

"Sorry, I don't mean to be rude, but . . . no, I won't participate with her."

Dada and Ms. Lipschultz looked at each other. Dada shrugged. I wondered how much I should tell them about the way Zippy bullied me after the mess in the lunchroom. The hurtful things she said didn't sting any longer. If she ever apologized, I could forgive her, but I wouldn't forget. And I would definitely not give her a shot at humiliating me again, especially not in front of the entire student body.

Ms. Lipschultz leaned forward, "Mango, it's too late to get another moderator, unless you have someone in mind."

"I do. I have two *someones* in mind: Izzy and Hailey Joanne. They're my best friends. They know me better than anyone else at the school."

"But . . . are you sure?"

"Yes, I am. I trust them."

"This is being recorded for television news. Do you think they might be nervous and freeze up?"

"Freeze up? Izzy? Have you ever seen her on stage?" I laughed. "And Hailey Joanne has more confidence than the oceans have fish."

Ms. Lipschultz buzzed her secretary, Ms. Pegg. "Locate Isabel Otero and Hailey Joanne Pinkney and have them brought to my office right away."

Izzy and Hailey Joanne were ecstatic when they found out they'd be onstage with TJ and me. Izzy immediately started dictating questions on her phone memo app. "I know exactly what to ask, because I know what the fans would like to know."

Hailey Joanne said, "I get to ask questions, too, Isabel, and not the kind of fan magazine puffball questions. I want the inside scoop, the behind-the-scenes exposé type of questions about the hard work and sacrifices you have to make as a star."

Ms. Lipschultz held up her hands, "All right, girls, let's remember, this is only for an hour, and you have to give the rest of the students a chance to participate."

Hailey Joanne cocked an eyebrow. "Of course. Don't sweat; we got this."

Ms. Lipschultz gave me a worried glance. I smiled and shrugged, they're my besties, and I was sure they'd do fine—but I had my fingers and toes crossed just in case.

I stood backstage with Dada listening to the kids react to scenes from the show. They were laughing at the jokes and cheering the songs. They were just as involved and excited as the live studio audiences had been. This was different though, because this was an audience of my real peers. A lot of them knew me from doing *Yo, Romeo!* together; some knew me from classes we shared; and others just by seeing me in the halls. The fact that they were reacting positively to the show made me feel grateful and proud. Zippy had said they were "fans, not friends." But I didn't care. Friends or fans, they made me feel good about myself, and I appreciated them.

Stepping out onto the Trueheart stage where it all began was incredible. I was so nostalgic that my eyes were wet with tears. All the kids were standing and cheering, and I was thinking how far I'd come since the first time I'd forced myself to step on this stage because Brooklyn had played a dirty trick by signing me up to audition when I'd had no intention of doing so. It turned out the trick backfired on her big time!

As I took my seat, I could feel Zippy's eyes glaring at me from the front row, as if trying to bore through my clothes and into my skin to inject me with venom. I smiled and winked at her. She knew very well why I had turned her down as the moderator; there was no need for an explanation. I was happy I had learned how to stand up for myself instead of accepting things I didn't want, just to avoid conflict.

When TJ appeared on screen from Los Angeles the auditorium erupted in cheers again. He looked great. We had been through so many ups and downs together, but the important thing was that we remained friends through it all. I knew that I could trust and count on TJ no matter what. That's what friendship is really about when it comes down to it—people you care about and who care about you, whether you're up or down, at your best or your worst. Friends are the ones you can turn to when you need advice, a shoulder to cry on, an ear to listen, or something as simple as a laugh or a good time. Building a true friendship takes time and work and maybe a little sacrifice, but it's truly worth it in the end.

Here I was, on the stage where it all began, with three people (two in person, one virtual) who I was sure would be a part of my journey for the rest of my life. Anyone else who wanted to be considered a friend would have a lot to live up to.

A gigantic sixteen-wheel moving truck arrived in front of our building early Saturday morning. As the movers lugged our furniture and boxes out of the apartment, Mom, Dada, Jasper, and I went around the building saying goodbye to the neighbors we had formed relationships with. Mrs. Kennedy, the lady we relied on so many times to take care of Jasper, cried. Mom gave her a her a bouquet of flowers, and Jasper hugged her neck really hard.

Just before leaving, I went back to my empty room for one last look. There were faded rectangles and tape marks on the walls where my posters had hung. The same fading on the inside of my closet door where my kissing-practice poster of Gabriel Faust had hung for the longest time. I thought back to the heart-to-heart talks Mom and I had shared in this room. Even though I was moving away, this room and the things that happened and the lessons I'd learned in here would always be a part of the core of what made me myself.

We were seated on the plane when I got a group text from TJ, Kashara, and Symphony.

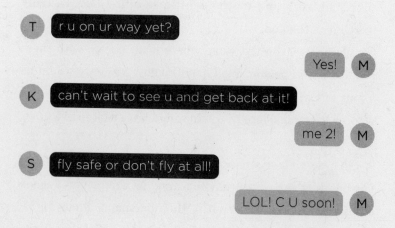

Mango All the Time

It was time to shut off all electronics, so I put my phone in airplane mode. Izzy, Hailey Joanne, and my dramanerd friends had taken a ton of pictures over the week. I opened my photo app and scrolled through them with a smile on my face. As the plane took off, I looked out the window as the city we were leaving behind fell farther and farther in the distance. When we were above the clouds and couldn't see the ground anymore, I sat back, closed my eyes, and opened my heart to all that was yet to come.

Acknowledgments

First and foremost, I would like to acknowledge my mother, Yvonne Blue Hyman Monroe, who passed away after suffering from dementia on the same day George Floyd's murder was made public. My mother was always a strong woman, and I drew on her strength to create Mango's mom, Marjorie.

When I was nine years old in the mid 1960s, we traveled from our home in Brooklyn, New York, to visit relatives in Wilson, North Carolina. We stayed at the Holiday Inn, which was very exciting for my sisters and me, who'd never even visited a hotel before. Mama took us to the outdoor swimming pool. When we got in, all the White people got out. My mother, who had grown up in Wilson at a time when she had to go to the back door at restaurants to get takeout food because Black people were not welcomed inside, was offended by the White retreat. She made my sisters and me stay in the pool all day to protest the ignorance of racism. We were pruned to the point of raisins and begged to get out, but no, we had to take a stand in the water. I value the strength and awareness of what it takes to be Black in America that she passed on to my sisters and me on that unforgettable day.

George Floyd's murder and the worldwide protests it ignited made me realize that I had to do something to pass on to Mango and her readers. A message about how Black Lives Matter and how to build the strength of character to stand up for what is right, fair, and just.

I am grateful to Sterling Publishing for supporting this book. At times, I worried that they would request that I pull back certain aspects, but that never happened. I owe so much to the most encouraging and supportive editor any author could ask for, Suzy Capozzi.

It takes a team to make an author look good on the page. Believe me, style and punctuation are not my forte, so I would like to "give props" to my team: Hannah Reich, our project editor, who oversaw the copyediting and proofreading; Gina Bonnano, our cover designer; Christine Heun, our interior designer; and Andrea Gochnauer, Blanca Oliviery, and Chris Vaccari, our sales and marketing team. I appreciate each and every one of you. Your hard work and support on behalf of *Mango* have been superior.

Big shout out to my brother from another mother as far as cover illustrations go; although we've never met, I have big love for you, Frank Morrison.

Gratitude to my agent, Kevin O'Connor, for your continued support and patience.

Last, but definitely not least, I owe everything to my husband, Ricaldo Rhoden, and our daughter, Jamaya Blue

Acknowledgments

Rhoden-Hyman. You put up with me writing in the kitchen, the den, the porch, everywhere but my own office. Your love, patience, and encouragement have seen me through the worst of times, and I love you so.

FRACASWELL HYMAN is an award-winning television writer, screenwriter, and actor. He is also a playwright, theater and television director, and producer who has created and executive-produced successful live-action animated television series (*The Famous Jett Jackson*, *Romeo*, and *Taina*), for Disney and Nickelodeon, earning him Peabody, Alma, and Humanitas awards. And his Netflix educational web series, *Bookmarks*, received a Kidscreen Award in 2021.

Fracaswell lives with his family in Wilmington, North Carolina, and can be found online at fracaswellhyman.com and on Instagram @fracaswell.